What Kids Say About Carole Marsh Mysteries . . .

I love the real locations! Reading the book always makes me want to go and visit them all on our next family vacation. My Mom says maybe, but I can't wait!

One day, I want to be a real kid in one of Ms. Marsh's mystery books. I think it would be fun, and I think I am a real character anyway. I filled out the application and sent it in and am keeping my fingers crossed!

History was not my favorite subject till I started reading Carole Marsh Mysteries. Ms. Marsh really brings history to life. Also, she leaves room for the scary and fun.

I think Christina is so smart and brave. She is lucky to be in the mystery books because she gets to go to a lot of places. I always wonder just how much of the book is true and what is made up. Trying to figure that out is fun!

Grant is cool and funny! He makes m

I like that there are boys and girls in *mysteries I outgrow, but I can always* *identify with in these books.*

They are scary, but not too scary. They are funny. I learn a lot.
There is always food which makes me hungry. I feel like I am there.

What Adults Say About Carole Marsh Mysteries . . .

I think kids love these books because they have such a wealth of detail.
I know I learn a lot reading them! It's an engaging way to look at the
history of any place or event. I always say I'm only going to read one
chapter to the kids, but that never happens—it's always two or three, at
least! —Librarian

Reading the mystery and going on the field trip—Scavenger Hunt in
hand—was the most fun our class ever had! It really brought the place
and its history to life. They loved the real kids characters and all the
humor. I loved seeing them learn that reading is an experience to
enjoy! —4th grade teacher

Carole Marsh is really on to something with these unique mysteries.
They are so clever; kids want to read them all. The Teacher's Guides
are chock full of activities, recipes, and additional fascinating
information. My kids thought I was an expert on the subject—and
with this tool, I felt like it! —3rd grade teacher

My students loved writing their own Real Kids/Real Places mystery
book! Ms. Marsh's reproducible guidelines are a real jewel. They
learned about copyright and more & ended up with their own book
they were so proud of! —Reading/Writing Teacher

The Mystery at the
KENTUCKY
DERBY

by
Carole Marsh

Published by Gallopade International/Carole Marsh Books. Printed in the United States of America.

Editorial Assistant: Steven St. Laurent; Cover design: Steven St. Laurent and Vicki DeJoy; Editor: Jenny Corsey; Graphic Design, layout and footer design: Steven St. Laurent; Photography: Steven St. Laurent.

Also available:
The Mystery at the Kentucky Derby Teacher's Guide

Gallopade is proud to be a member of these educational organizations and associations:

International Reading Association
National Association for Gifted Children
The National School Supply and Equipment Association
Association for Supervision and Curriculum Development
The National Council for the Social Studies
Museum Store Association
Association of Partners for Public Lands

NSSEA

This book is dedicated to a little girl named Ellen Grace, for whom everything is horsey-this and horsey-that.
And every day when her daddy gets home, the first thing he hears is, "Daddy, can you be a horsey?!"

For additional information on Carole Marsh Mysteries, visit:
www.carolemarshmysteries.com

Horse Snort!

20 YEARS AGO . . .

As a mother and an author, one of the fondest periods of my life was when I decided to write mystery books for children. At this time (1979) kids were pretty much glued to the TV, something parents and teachers complained about the way they do about video games today.

I decided to set each mystery in a real place—a place kids could go and visit for themselves after reading the book. And I also used real children as characters. Usually a couple of my own children served as characters, and I had no trouble recruiting kids from the book's location to also be characters.

Also, I wanted all the kids—boys and girls of all ages—to participate in solving the mystery. And, I wanted kids to learn something as they read. Something about the history of the location. And I wanted the stories to be funny.

That formula of real+scary+smart+fun served me well. The kids and I had a great time visiting each site and many of the events in the stories actually came out of our experiences there. (For example, we really did stay at a horse farm outside Louisville, go to the Kentucky Derby Museum and the Falls of the Ohio, see the Pegasus Parade, get snorted on by a horse, and have many more adventures in the Louisville area!)

I love getting letters from teachers and parents who say they read the book with their class or child, then visited the historic site and saw all the places in the mystery for themselves. What's so great about that? What's great is that you and your children have an experience that bonds you together forever. Something you shared. Something you both cared about at the time. Something that crossed all age levels—a good story, a good scare, a good laugh!

20 years later,

Carole Marsh

Christina Yother   **Grant Yother**   **Sara Knox**   **Tanner Knox**

About the Characters

Christina Yother, 9, from Peachtree City, Georgia

Grant Yother, 7, from Peachtree City, Georgia, Christina's brother

Tanner Knox, age 12, from Newnan, Georgia, as Tanner from Louisville, KY. Tanner's Dad does have a horse farm!

Sara Knox, age 10, from Newnan, Georgia, Tanner's cousin, from Louisville, KY. Reesie, the pony she rides in the story, is really hers!

The many places featured in the book actually exist and are worth a visit! Perhaps you could read the book and follow the trail these kids went on during their mysterious adventure!

TITLES IN THE CAROLE MARSH MYSTERIES SERIES

Books and Teacher's Guides are available at booksellers, libraries, school supply stores, museums, and many other locations!

CONTENTS

1 Thoroughbreds in the Mist

A thick, swirling fog hung low over the ground in the cool air of the pre-dawn darkness. The rich moisture had settled on every surface. Billions of tiny droplets reflected what little light penetrated the fog. The fence rail where Christina and Grant stood stretched away to their left. Eerily glistening in the bluish light from the Churchill Downs grandstand, the railing faded away into the fog.

Christina and Grant peered through the mist at the wide expanse of dirt between the outside and inside rail. Across the track, near the big white column that marked the finish line, stood three men. Their dark silhouettes were punctuated by the blue-green glow of a digital stopwatch.

The sound of a lone horse at full gallop came from far in the distance, the hoofbeats muted by the mist.

"He's entering the third turn," Sara said quietly.

Christina, nine years old, turned away from the track to look at Sara, the ten-year-old daughter of Mimi's friend. Mimi, Christina's grandmother, had brought her and her brother Grant to Louisville, Kentucky for the 130th running of the Kentucky Derby.

"How do you know?" Christina asked. She rubbed her arms to rid them of the creepy goosebumps.

"The hoofbeats stopped moving away from us," Sara explained.

"Wow! You've got good hearing!" Grant, Christina's seven-year-old brother, whispered excitedly.

"It's creepy sometimes," said Tanner, Sara's twelve-year-old cousin. "You can't sneak up on her."

"Shh!" Sara hissed. "Quarter-mile," she said, and stood up to grip the wet rail.

Tanner moved up beside her, and the four of them focused on the fogged-up Home Stretch. Some called this short 1/4-mile-long patch of dirt Heartbreak Lane, because it was where the Kentucky Derby was really won or lost.

The hoofbeats grew louder as the horse raced up the home stretch. The gallop became faster as the invisible horse put forth a final surge of speed.

Then, as if caught in slow-motion mid-stride and seeming to float on the fog, the horse and jockey burst into sight. Curls of fog swirled in the horse's wake like the tentacles of a ghostly octopus. Dirt flew up from the horse's hoof steps in shadowy globs.

The horse passed the finish line and flew by the four kids in a streak of dark hair and yellow silk. Christina watched the horse and jockey disappear into the fogbank as the gallop began to slow down.

Grant giggled excitedly. "Oh, man!" he exclaimed. "That was fast!"

"Not fast enough," Tanner said.

"What do you mean?" Christina asked.

"What's his time?" Sara asked.

Tanner held up his stopwatch for them to see. Black numbers floated in the blue-green glow: 2:09.13.

"Two minutes, nine point one-three seconds," Sara moaned. "That *is* slow."

"If that's slow," Grant began, "then what's *fast*?"

"The closer to two minutes, the better," Sara explained. "That—" she pointed at the stopwatch— "is seven seconds off the average time to win the Derby."

Christina peered down the track past Tanner and Sara as the racehorse cantered back toward the finish line and

the three men. It was a dreamy, fairy tale-like sight. The horse's dark shape glided through the mist at a trot's pace, with the jockey sitting tall on his back. The yellow silk of his shirt and the horse's saddlecloth shimmered in the light from the grandstand.

After a minute, the jockey turned the Thoroughbred back down the track, and they trotted off. Two of the three men disappeared into the fog over the infield, but one had hopped over the inside rail and was approaching them.

"Is that your Dad?" Christina asked Sara.

"It is," Sara replied. "And I'll bet he's disappointed. Skit usually runs fast in the morning."

"Hiyo, kids," Sara's Dad called. "Whatcha think? Have we got a winner, or what?"

"I'll bet you do," Grant said happily. "That horse is fast!"

"Looks good to me," Christina chimed in.

"Hmmm," Tanner hummed skeptically.

"He was slow this morning, Dad," Sara said sadly.

"That's okay," Dad said. "We were trying something a little different in the running."

"I guess it didn't work," Sara said.

"Not the way we expected," Dad replied. They fell silent as the sound of a starting bell pierced through the foggy darkness. The hoofbeats of another horse making an

early morning run quickly blurred from a trot to a canter to a gallop. Christina and Grant scooted away from the rail so Sara's Dad could jump over.

The horse streaked by and disappeared into the fog, its hoofbeats quickly fading.

An electronic tone chirped from the wireless phone on Sara's Dad's waist.

"*Charles...*" a hurried voice said.

Charles lifted the phone to his mouth. "What is it, Earl?"

"*We need you in the stable,*" Earl said anxiously. "*Lickety-Split is pitching a fit. He's been going on since before we got back—screaming and kicking up a storm. Something's got him spooked!*"

2 TROUBLE AT THE STABLES

"Whoa, boy! Easy! Drew! Grab that rope!" Earl yelled.

In the background, they could all hear a horse squealing. "He's scared," Charles said into the phone. "Is there anyone else around?"

"Not close by," Earl said. *"I think there are a couple of crews warming up on the other side of the stables, but this side's quiet."*

"Well, see if you can get him into his trailer to calm him down. I'll be there in five," Charles said. He clipped the now silent phone back to his waist.

"I've got to get over there," Charles said to the kids. "Want to come see the stables?"

"I'd love to see the stables," Christina said.

"Sure, Mister—" Grant started. "Uhh... I can't remember your family name!"

"Grant," Sara's Dad said, laying a hand on Grant's

7

shoulder, "please, please call me Charles."

Grant scrunched his eyebrows, then shrugged and nodded an okay. He wasn't used to calling an adult by his first name. Mimi and Papa always insisted on "Mr. Him" and "Mrs. Her"—and always "Yes, ma'am" and "No, sir."

Charles turned on his heel and led them toward the stables on the other side of the track.

"Who's Lickety-Split?" Grant asked.

"That's our lead pony," Sara answered.

"What's a lead pony?" Christina asked.

"Everybody uses lead ponies to escort the racehorses to the gate," Tanner said. "The lead pony is there to help keep the racehorse calm. It's pretty noisy at post time!"

"Sounds like it's a little backwards right now," Charles said. "The racehorse is going to calm down his pony."

"What's post time?" Grant asked.

"That's when they play that tune on a bugle," Christina replied. "It's called the Call to the Post."

"Oh, yeaaah!" Grant crooned, as he remembered the tune. He curled both hands into hollow fists and held them end-to-end in front of his mouth, like a bugler. "Brrp-b-t-brrp-b-t-brrp-b-t-brrp-b-t-brrrrpp..." he played before Christina told him to hush.

"Who's Earl?" Christina asked.

"He's our trainer," Charles answered. "One of the best trainers in horse racing."

"Drew is his assistant," Sara said.

The foggy black of night had slowly turned to a dark, dull gray by the time they reached the stables. Charles led them past several buildings before they entered one end of a brightly lit stable that smelled of freshly laid hay. Charles slipped into a small office near the entrance. Sara walked on ahead, peering into each stall.

It was quiet. Almost too quiet. There was none of the squealing and whinnying they had heard just minutes ago.

"Where did everyone go?" Tanner asked.

"Fritz and Skit aren't here," Sara reported. "But they might still be cooling off."

"Who's Fritz?" Grant wanted to know. He was unusually full of questions this early in the morning. "And who's Skit?"

"Fritz is our jockey," Sara explained as she walked past them, heading for the office.

"And Skit is the racehorse's nickname," Tanner finished. "His official, registered Jockey Club name is—"

BANG!!!!!

3 WHEN PLANS BACKFIRE

The loud noise shattered the silence of the dawn! Everyone jumped at the loud sound. Christina snatched a wide-eyed Grant away from the entrance to the stable and backed into an empty stall.

Charles exploded from the office, accidentally knocking Sara and Tanner to the floor in a tangle of arms and legs as he left the stable. Tanner scrambled to his feet and darted to the entrance. He peered out into the fog.

"What's going on, Tia?" Grant whispered.

"I don't know, Grant," she whispered back.

"Was that a gunshot?" Grant asked.

"I don't know," Christina said.

They strained their ears to listen and heard a truck's engine racing away. They heard horses in the nearby

11

stables whinnying nervously, having been rudely awoken by the loud bang.

Then they heard men's voices. They were speaking in angry tones, their words fast and short. Christina and Grant just couldn't hear them well enough to understand what they were saying.

"Here they come," Tanner said, backing away from the door.

Charles appeared in the doorway, supporting another man on his shoulders. The man's clothes had been dirtied, and one sleeve of his jacket was torn.

"C'mon, Earl," Charles said, "let's get you into the infirmary."

Earl was holding a hand to his forehead. As they passed, he lowered it to his jacket pocket to get a towel. Christina gasped as they all saw the bloody gash on Earl's forehead. It seemed as if the whole right side of his face was coated in blood.

"Eeeewww!" Sara cried.

"Whoa!" Grant exclaimed. "Did you see that?" he said to Tanner.

"Yeah! I bet that hurt," Tanner said, and he followed Charles and Earl further into the stable and through a set of doors.

"Let's go," Grant said, and he headed out of the stall and right for the doors to the infirmary.

"Grant!" Christina called.

"Wait!" Sara cried.

"What?" Grant said, as he turned around.

"We can't go in there," Christina said.

"Why not? It's safer in there with the adults," Grant said, and he turned back around. He knew she could not argue with that reasoning.

Christina and Sara glanced at each other, then followed him into the infirmary.

Earl sat on the edge of a big metal table—big enough to hold a horse. Christina and Sara entered the room just in time to see Charles swipe a huge glop of some kind of yucky green ointment over the gash on poor Earl's head.

"Ewww!" Christina cried. "What's that?"

"It stops the bleeding," Charles answered, as he grabbed for some sterile cloths. He gently wiped away the blood from around Earl's wound.

"Where's Skit?" Sara asked. "And Fritz?"

"I don't know," Charles answered. "Drew went to go find them."

"Where's Lickety-Split?" Tanner asked.

Charles stopped wiping. "He's—"

"Charles! Earl!" a voice cried.

"In here, Drew!" Charles called back.

The doors to the infirmary swung open, and a tall out-of-breath young man with seriously messed up blond hair burst in.

"Skit and Fritz are okay," he said, trying to catch his breath.

"They were cooling off," he gasped. "They'll be back here any minute now."

"Do you know who that was?" Charles asked. "Who drove off with our truck?"

Drew now had his hands on his knees to support his hunched-over frame. He shook his head, no.

"I didn't get a good look. Someone wrapped a towel around my head and gave me a good knock on the noggin'."

Earl groaned on the table. "Must have been the same fella who clunked me on the head. And stole my keys."

Charles went back to wiping the blood off Earl's face.

"Tell me exactly what happened," he said. Christina could hear the anger in his voice. She could tell, though, that he was very good at keeping it under control.

"We finally got Lickety to stay on all fours," Earl began. "It took a minute, but we got him calmed. We took him out to the trailer—Skit's trailer—and loaded him in."

Earl moaned again. He held his head up with one hand and said, "My head really hurts."

"He was real calm after that," Drew continued. "He let us tie him up like normal. We had just closed the gate when it happened."

"When what happened?" Charles demanded.

"Well, this guy wrapped a towel around my head and knocked me out—hit me on the back of my head with something..." Drew paused and gingerly placed a hand atop his head. "The next thing I know, somebody's shootin' at us!"

"That wasn't a gun, Drew," Earl said. "The truck backfired when he shifted gears."

"Earl? What happened to you?" Charles asked.

Earl looked up. He shook his head. "I turned around when I heard Drew get clunked, and all I see is this shadow swingin' a two-by-four or somethin' at me. Got me right here..." Earl pointed at the gooey gash.

Christina shivered. At least Charles had wiped all the blood away, Christina thought.

"That didn't stop him, though," Earl went on. "That first swing got me good, but not good enough. Soon as I was stupid enough to try and get back up, I got clunked again. I couldn't move until you picked me up, Charles."

Charles put the blood-soaked towels in a bright red bin labeled Bio-Hazardous Waste. "I think you'll live," he said, "but I'm calling for an ambulance just in case you've got a concussion."

Christina, Grant, Sara, and Tanner watched in anticipation as Charles sat down on the table next to Earl. He plucked his phone off his belt and dialed 9-1-1.

Just seconds later, he said, "Yes, officer, I need an ambulance—and I need to report a horse-napping!"

4 A STATE OF HEIGHTENED MYSTERY

A little over an hour later, Christina and Grant sat high atop a stack of hay bales and sipped their hot chocolate—made with milk, not water! Tanner and Sara sat below them with their own steaming mugs. The lingering fog was beginning to burn away in the rising sunlight, but it was still pretty thick. Thick enough, anyway, to nearly hide the flashing lights of the police cars and the ambulance.

A lone horse stood behind them, munching the grass in its enclosure. Christina would occasionally turn and watch it. *That horse has been moving closer and closer to us,* she thought. *Ever since we sat down—now it's only... maybe... as far from home plate as first base is? Hmmm...*

Grant sighed. "I hope we still get to the Great Steamboat Race," he said. Grant fiddled with the Churchill Downs V.I.P. Pass that he wore around his neck on a dogtag

17

chain. The others wore similar Passes.

"I'm sure we will," Christina said. "It's not like this is a mystery *we* can solve."

"Huh?" Tanner grunted. "What do you mean? It's not a mystery *you* can solve?"

"Yeah, Tanner!" Grant said. "We solve mysteries! All across America!"

Sara just looked at him. "Yeah, yeah, Grant. Sure."

"It's true!" Grant cried. "Tell 'em, Tia!"

Christina told Tanner and Sara about some of the mysterious events into which she and her brother had gotten swept in the past.

"Like, just last year," Christina explained, "we were in New York City for the Fourth of July, and somebody stole the original torch from the Statue of Liberty—"

"—but we were the only ones who knew!" Grant added.

"And at Christmas last year," Christina continued, "we were at the White House—"

"In Washington, D.C.?" Tanner asked.

"Yes!" Christina replied, "and nobody could find the President in the middle of a blizzard!"

Grant giggled. "And I was running all over the White House in my underwear!" He giggled and giggled and nearly spilled his hot chocolate.

"And that's not all!" Christina said, almost as excited as Grant. "This runs in the family!"

"Our Mom and her brother used to do this mystery stuff, too!" Grant added.

"Yeah! This one time, they were in Bath, North Carolina for the Blackbeard Play, and—"

"Oh, no! What have you kids done this time?!" a concerned, familiar voice said, startling them from their chocolate-and-flashing-lights-induced trance.

"Papa!" Grant exclaimed. He turned so fast that hot chocolate splashed out of his mug and onto his leg. "Ouch!"

"What's going on here, kids?" Mimi asked. "Why are the police and EMTs here? Are any of you hurt?"

Christina carefully put her mug down on a fencepost behind the hay bales before she made any sudden moves. She joined Grant, who climbed off the bales to hug Mimi and Papa.

She heard the horse in the pen neigh.

"We've had a kidnapping," she said as she greeted them.

"A *horse*-napping," Grant corrected, as he dabbed at his pants with a towel.

Papa's eyes nearly popped out of their sockets in surprise. Mimi's jaw dropped.

"Which horse?" Papa, Mimi's husband, wanted to know.

"Lickety-Split," Sara answered.

"How on earth did that happen?" Mimi asked.

Grant clambered back up on the bales as Christina filled them in on the events of the last couple of hours. She wrapped up her account with one bit of speculation...

"The catch is, Lickety-Split was driven away in Skit's trailer. I think that whoever stole Lickety-Split thinks they really stole Skit. They've got a lead pony when they think they have a racehorse!"

Mimi—her mystery-writing mind now in Mystery Mode—nodded in agreement. "That sounds quite possible. I just wonder what might happen if and when they find out that they've got the wrong horse!"

"Now," Papa said, raising a finger, "I'm confused. How does somebody steal the wrong horse while thinking they stole the right one?"

"Skit and Lickety-Split are the same color, chestnut," Sara answered. "Skit is a little short for a Thoroughbred, and Lickety-Split is tall for a pony."

"Ohhh," Papa said. "So Skit is the racehorse I've heard so much about? The one called—"

"Friends!" a man called. "You made it!"

Charles approached the group and shook Papa's hand, then gave Mimi a big hug and a kiss on each cheek. Mimi blushed till her cheeks were as red as roses.

Christina heard the horse neigh again. It was even closer now.

"Did you enjoy your sleep? Was the cabin warm enough?" Mimi and Papa had spent the night in one of the guest cabins at Charles's horse farm—the legendary Swamp Fox Farm.

They nodded politely and thanked him for being so generous, especially for the real country breakfast—farm-fresh eggs (over easy), fresh bacon (cut just the day before), grits (*not* the instant kind), toast with fresh creamery butter, and coffee and OJ—cooked for them right in their cabin by a personal chef!

Grant arched an eyebrow as Mimi described their wonderful breakfast and kept right on talking to Charles. His mouth started to water. His tummy started to rumble. Grant arched his other eyebrow and said, "Oh, man! I'm hungry!"

"Grant, is food all you can think about?" Christina asked.

Grant nodded. "That breakfast sounded real good!"

"It's all I can think about right now," Tanner said, rubbing his tummy.

Sara and Christina looked at each other and rolled their eyes. "BOYS!" they moaned.

The horse neighed, as if to agree with them. It's only about 30 feet away now, Christina thought. "Why don't you finish your hot chocolate," she suggested.

Grant whinnied. "I can't! I spilled some of it when Papa surprised me, and then—well, I guess I knocked my cup over." He looked around for the Kentucky Derby mug he'd been drinking from.

"Grrrrant!" Christina growled. "There's more hot chocolate in the stable. Where's your cup? I'll get it for you."

Grant was still looking. "I can't find it!" he cried, trying to move the loose bales so he could see in the gaps.

"Did it fall behind you?" Sara asked.

The horse neighed again. It had crept closer.

Grant looked down at the ground behind the stack of hay bales. There, lying in the thick, green, unmowed grass between the hay and a fence, lay his mug.

"There it is!" he exclaimed. He jumped off the bales and over the fence in one motion. He didn't notice the horse.

Christina climbed back up on the bales to get her hot chocolate.

"Got it!" he called.

"Hand it to me, Grant," Christina said, and she stretched out her arm.

"Whoa, Nellie!" Grant cried. "What's this?!"

5 SOWING THE SEEDS OF... A MYSTERY!

Grant's head appeared over the white fence's top rail. His blue eyes were wide with excitement. His little mouth was open in amazement.

"I think it's a clue," he whispered to Christina.

Grant held up a folded piece of paper. "It's got writing on it!" he proclaimed.

"Let me see it!" Christina demanded.

"I found it, so I'm reading it first," Grant said. He gently unfolded the paper, as if it would crumble to pieces if he touched it wrong.

Christina watched his lips move as he read.

He nodded wisely, then said, "Yup, it's a clue!" Then he handed the paper to his sister, satisfied that he had read the clue first.

Christina looked at the slip of paper. It had a Race

23

Number on it, and numbers next to the words Win, Place, and Show. A betting slip, she thought. But what interested Christina was the message handwritten with a felt-tip pen:

Eva Bandman Park — 6:00 p.m. Wed.
Bring Polaroid photo of the horse in his trailer.

"Boy, somebody needs to work on their penmanship," Sara said, taking the slip from Christina and reading it.

"This might be a note from one thief to the another," Christina said. "Where's Eva Bandman Park?"

"It's on the Ohio River," Tanner said. "It's a great spot to watch the Great Steamboat Race. Also, there's Waterfront Park, where the race starts and ends. Then you have Twin Park, Cox Park, and even Riverfront Park, across the river in Jeffersonville, Indiana."

"The race is being held today!" Sara whispered excitedly. "It starts at 5:00 p.m., I think."

"We're going to be there," Grant said. "But maybe not at that park! Oh, no!"

"How can we make sure that we go to Eva Bandman Park?" Christina asked.

She looked at Sara. Sara looked at Grant. Grant looked at Tanner, as if he certainly had the answer. Tanner gulped.

"Umm... well, this year, there's a Ferris wheel and some other carnival rides at Eva Bandman Park," Tanner suggested. "It's the last time Derby Festival planners will be able to—the city is going to tear up all the soccer and rugby fields. They're going to turn the whole park into a nature conservation area for the Louisville Zoo."

Christina thought about that. There was a Ferris wheel there. Mimi had a passion for Ferris wheels—she had to ride nearly every one she saw. Christina felt confident that they would be going to Eva Bandman Park to watch the Great Steamboat Race!

"There's more, Christina," Grant said.

"More paper?" Christina asked. She looked up, and realized that the horse was standing right behind Grant!

"No, more clue," Grant replied. "There's a pile of sunflower seed shells down here." The horse snorted and tapped Grant's head with his nose.

"YIPE!" Grant yelped as his hair was blown around and he got an earful of horse snort. He jumped up on the fence and climbed back up on top of the hay bales.

Suddenly, they all jumped as Charles' voice startled them. "Hey! What's going on over here?" Charles said. "Sara? What do you have?"

Christina's eyed popped open in surprise. The clue!

They had never lost a clue before! She watched in despair as the creased slip of paper passed from Sara's hand to her father's hand.

"Where did you find this?" he asked after reading the note. He looked at all four kids. His eyes locked onto Grant. Grant managed to stare back for a few seconds. But he couldn't stand the pressure.

"I-I found it, sir!" Grant stammered. "It was lying in the grass over there." He pointed to a spot on the ground far away from where he had found the slip and the seeds.

Charles looked where Grant pointed, but he couldn't really see the spot behind the bales of hay. "Hmm," he grunted. He tucked the paper into his shirt pocket, then nodded.

"Folks," Charles said, "here's the situation: Lickety-Split, our lead pony, has been horse-napped. Lickety-Split and Skit look very similar, and Skit's own black-and-tan trailer was stolen. Those clues lead us to believe that the thieves *think* they stole Skit."

"The media will not be told that our horse was stolen," Charles continued. "The police and I think it would be best if the thieves continue to think they have Skit. It will buy us time to figure out what they want and time to find Lickety-Split. So, no one says nothing to nobody about this, okay?"

Everyone nodded in agreement.

Charles then wished them a good day of sightseeing, then thanked the kids for finding the note. He excused himself and walked back to the police cars.

"What did you find, Grant?" Papa asked.

"Uhh... I'm not sure," Grant said.

"I think it was a betting slip," Christina offered. Sara nodded in agreement.

"It wasn't a clue or anything?" Mimi asked with a mischievous little smile.

"No, ma'am," Christina said. "Just 1 to Show, 2 to Place and 3 to Win!"

Papa chuckled. "That's a pretty good day at the track!"

"What are we going to do now, Mimi?" Grant asked.

Mimi put on the mischievous smile again. "Want to go see a movie? One that's not just surround sound, but surround sight, too?!"

"YES, MA'AM!" Grant shouted in excitement.

The horse whinnied at Grant. Grant jumped down off the bales of hay. "You... horse!" Grant said.

"Well, all right, then!" Papa said. "We're off to the Kentucky Derby Museum!"

"Yip-yip-yippee!" Grant yipped. "But, Papa?"

"Yes?"

"I'm starving! Can we get some breakfast first?"

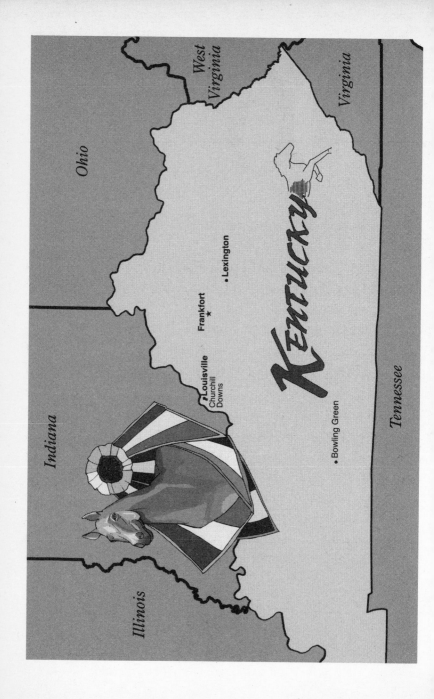

6 QUIZ TIME!

"Wow! That was exciting, wasn't it?" Mimi asked the four kids as they piled into Charles' giant SUV. They had just finished a tour of the Kentucky Derby Museum. It was conveniently located right there at Churchill Downs.

Christina—and everyone else—felt that the highlight of the tour was definitely "The Greatest Race." The movie was displayed on a 360-degree screen that wrapped all the way around the theater. It put them right in the middle of all the action on Kentucky Derby Day. After it was over, Mimi said that she could have stayed in there all day to watch it over and over and over again.

Now, Christina heaved a big bag of books up into the truck. Mimi had gone horse-crazy in the museum's gift shop, buying all sorts of books and Kentucky Derby memorabilia. Many of them were for Mimi's mystery

research—she was going to write a mystery about horse racing. But she had also bought a bunch for Christina and Grant.

"So, where to next?" Papa asked.

"I was thinking we could go to the Louisville Slugger Museum," Mimi said. "We can spend part of the afternoon there, then get a picnic lunch, and go find a good spot on the riverfront to watch the Great Steamboat Race!"

"That sounds like a wonderful idea!" Grant said, and he hopped up into the truck.

"Let's go check out some baseball bats!" Tanner said. He and Sara were sitting in the third-row seats.

Papa drove off while Mimi read the map and gave directions. After she was absolutely sure that Papa knew which way to go, Mimi turned around in her seat and said, "Quiz time!"

All the kids groaned.

"Quiz time?" Grant moaned. "Oh, why, oh why, oh why?"

"So that you can make sure you remember things you just saw and read about at the Derby Museum," Mimi said. "Now—who's first? Grant, you are! Can you tell me when the first Kentucky Derby was held?"

Grant stopped complaining about quiz time and thought

about it. "Eighteen... eighteen seventy... 1875!"

"Do you know who started it?" Mimi asked.

"I do!" Grant said happily. "Meriwether Lewis Clark... Junior!"

"Who was he the grandson of?"

"William Clark of the Lewis and Clark Corps of Discovery Expedition," Grant replied.

"Good! And why do they call it the 'Run for the Roses'?" Mimi asked.

"Ooh! Because they pile roses up on top of the horse that wins!" Grant replied proudly.

"Close," Mimi said. "It's actually a blanket of hundreds of roses." She looked around the cabin of the truck for the next Quiz Victim.

"Sara, you're next," Mimi said. Sara nodded that she was ready. "You, living here, should know this. Does every horse that wins a race at Churchill Downs visit the Winner's Circle?"

"No, ma'am," Sara replied. "Only the winners of the Kentucky Derby."

"Great! And... why do jockeys wear such colorful silk shirts?" Mimi asked.

"So you can tell which horse is which during a race," Sara answered smartly.

"Do you know when that started?" Papa asked. He sometimes joined in on the quizzes—Papa was like a walking encyclopedia of trivia.

Nobody knew the answer, so Papa answered his own question. "King Charles II of England started it when he began to hold racing events on the plains of Hempstead. All the princes, barons, and dukes couldn't tell which horse was which. So the King made each jockey wear a silk shirt of a different color. The colored silk actually stayed with the horse—or the horse's owner. So if a jockey rode a different horse, he wore a silk shirt of a different color. And they still do that today."

"Hey!" Mimi exclaimed. "Papa paid attention in the Museum!" She clapped her hands. "Bravo!"

Papa leaned forward in a bow.

"Okay, Christina, you're up!" Mimi said. "Are all the jockeys that ride in the Kentucky Derby men?"

Christina remembered studying a special exhibit about female jockeys. "Usually, the jockeys are men. But women *have* ridden in the race."

"Do you know how many?" Mimi asked.

"Not many," Christina replied. "I think, maybe four?"

"*Muy bien*," Mimi said in Spanish. Very good! "Have any won the Kentucky Derby?

"No—but Julie Krone, who rode in the Kentucky Derby twice, once won the Belmont Stakes!"

"Great! What about African American jockeys?"

Christina tried to remember—the African American jockey exhibit was right next to the women's. "Umm... none have ridden in the Kentucky Derby in over 100 years."

"Right!" Mimi said excitedly. "You're all doing so well! Now it's your turn, Tanner—do you know the name of the horse that won the first Kentucky Derby?"

"Yes, ma'am," Tanner replied. "Aristides was his name. His jockey was a black man."

"At 2-to-1 odds," Papa chimed in. "He was the favorite to win."

"What about last year's winner?"

"Funny Cide!" Grant shouted. He giggled. "Sorry! I couldn't help it!" he giggled some more. "It's a funny name!" he giggled on and on.

"All right, all right," Mimi said. "Do you know what the Triple Crown is, what races are included, and where they're held?"

"It's three races," Tanner said, "the Kentucky Derby, here in Louisville; the Preakness, in Baltimore, Maryland; and the Belmont Stakes, in Belmont Park, New York. It's a jockey's and owner's dream to win all three races!"

"Excellent! One last question: how many Triple Crown winners have there been, and who was the last Triple Crown winner?"

"There have been eleven Triple Crown winners, and Affirmed was the last—in 1978," Tanner finished.

"That's great, kids," Papa said. "Every one right."

"That's incredible!" Mimi said. "Okay... I'm going to sit back and see the sights!"

"Me too!" said Grant. He kicked off his shoes and crossed his legs up on the seat.

"I hope your feet don't stink, Grant," Sara said.

"Hey! My feet don't stink!" Grant said.

Christina thought that he looked as if he could fall asleep any second. They had gotten up soooo early this morning. She also thought, I could probably fall asleep any second, too!

It was silent in the truck, except for the bluegrass tunes playing softly on the radio. Christina kicked off her shoes, too, and got more comfortable in her seat. She listened to the sound of the music and the hum of the SUV's engine, and she watched the city of Louisville slide past her window.

There's an awful lot of horse stuff around here, Christina thought. An *awful* lot. And that got her thinking

about Lickety-Split, the poor missing pony.

Why on earth would anyone steal a horse, she thought. I guess if it's a winning racehorse, a Thoroughbred, it could be worth lots of money. Hundreds of thousands of dollars, she thought, maybe even millions!

But where would you take it? A farm, silly! Christina remembered from the Official State of Kentucky Travel Guide that there were hundreds of horse farms outside Louisville. They might never find that poor horse!

But we have two clues to work with, Christina thought. One, the betting slip with the meeting time and place. Two, the sunflower seeds. Whoever left that pile of shells with the betting slip was a sunflower seed nut!

That made her sleepy mind think of Mr. Peanut. I think I'll call the thief Mr. Sunflower Seed, Christina thought.

Christina was very worried about Lickety-Split. I hope they feed him, she thought, suddenly very saddened by the theft of the lead pony.

Her eyelids grew heavier and heavier, and the soft, gentle vibrations of the SUV soon had Christina, Grant, Sara, and Tanner fast asleep.

7 THE OHIO RIVER IS FALLING!

The sound of the SUV's doors closing woke Christina up. She opened her eyes, then closed them right back—the sun was pouring in her window. Christina turned her head and opened her eyes again. Grant was sitting next to her, sleepily trying to get his shoes back on. A glance into the back seat revealed Tanner and Sara waking up as well.

Mimi opened Christina's door. "Come on out, kids. We have just enough time to see the Falls of the Ohio before we HAVE to get back across the river and find a spot for our picnic."

"I thought we were going to the Louisville Slugger Museum," Grant whined, as Papa opened his door.

"We were, Grant," Papa began, "but everybody fell asleep. So we drove around Louisville for about an hour. Mimi took pictures of a lot of historic sites."

"And some that aren't so historic," Mimi said, "but will make some interesting pictures!"

Christina asked, "Mimi, what did you take pictures of?"

"Well, let's see," Mimi said, "I wrote down my subjects on a note pad—where is it? Oh, let's see if I can remember... I took pictures of the 'haunted' J.B. Speed House—and later picked up some literature from the J.B. Speed Art Museum."

"Who's J.B. Speed?" Grant asked.

"He was a generous man who founded the J.B. Speed Art Museum," Papa said.

"Oh—so he was an anthropologist," Grant said.

Mimi and Papa laughed. "No, Grant, he was a *philanthropist.*"

"Anyway," Mimi continued, "I also took pictures of the Conrad/Caldwell House and Museum, and the Filson Club and Historical Society Museum."

"Who were they?" Christina asked.

"Theophilus Conrad was a Frenchman who made a ton of money in the tanning business back in the late 1800s," Papa explained.

"They had tanning beds back then?" Grant asked, surprised.

"No, no, no," Tanner moaned. "Conrad was a tanner. They took hides from cattle, bison, horses, just about any

big animal, and treated them so that the leather could be used for furniture, clothing, saddles, and lots of other stuff."

"Oh!" Grant said.

"What about Filson?" Christina asked.

"I know!" Sara exclaimed. "John Filson was Louisville's first historian. He and a bunch of friends got together at the Durrett House and founded the Filson Club. It was nine men who met at the house to read papers about Kentucky history, drink crab-apple cider, and smoke Filson cigars. My dad's a member of the Filson Historical Society, so I've read a lot about our local history."

"That's a good bit of trivia, Sara," Mimi said, proudly.

Grant looked out at the Falls as they walked towards the Interpretive Center.

"Those Falls don't look like they're falling anywhere," he said. "They're pretty flat. I thought we were going to see a real big waterfall."

Christina had read about the Falls in school. "Grant, they're more like rapids," she informed him. "It takes over two miles for them to drop the Ohio River just 26 feet. They're more known for their rich fossil beds—just wait till you see the exhibits!"

"Very good, Christina!" Mimi exclaimed. "Oh, look, here we are."

They had reached the doors to the Falls of the Ohio Interpretive Center. Papa opened one door and held it open as everyone in the group passed through.

"This place looks like it was carved out of the rocks in the southwest United States," Tanner said, commenting on the striped façade of the building.

Mimi told them to spread out and study the exhibits. Each had to remember five facts about the Falls—and there would be another Quiz Time when they got back to the car.

Christina, Grant, Sara, and Tanner explored the exhibits for quite some time. Mimi finally gathered them together for a quick photo shoot. She hustled them outside and snapped a few pictures of the four kids, with the Falls in the background.

"All right, Quiz Time!" Mimi announced when they were all back in the truck and buckled up. "Christina, start at the beginning and tell us about the early history of the Falls."

Christina cleared her throat and began. "Ahem... the parking lot we're now in was once at the bottom of a shallow tropical ocean, kind of like the Caribbean Sea. More than 350 million years ago, this land wasn't even here, geographically speaking."

"Where was it?" Papa asked.

click!

Falls of the Ohio

"Somewhere near the earth's equator," Christina replied. "It was long before the continents separated and arranged themselves where they are now. It was even long before dinosaurs were running around."

"Great," Mimi said. "Tanner... what is that time called, and what happened, geologically speaking?"

"It's the geological period called the Devonian Period," Tanner replied. "All the land masses that are now continents were still moving toward a big Supercontinent. Then, maybe 100 million years later, they were all connected, and the ocean drained away."

"I can NOT imagine continents just getting up and moving around the world!" Grant said in amazement. "That must have made a LOT of noise!"

"It took millions of years, Grant," Christina said. "They move very slowly. And they're still moving. Some parts may move less than an inch every 100 years, but some might move a whole foot in that time."

"When they move a lot at once, we have an earthquake," Sara said.

"Okay, okay," Mimi interrupted. "Tanner, what else happened during the Devonian Period, and then afterward?"

"Fish began to appear in great numbers—especially in

the tropical ocean that was here. There was a lot of plant life... amphibians were starting to appear—"

"Frogs and toads!" Grant cried. "Ribbit! Ribbit!"

"Then the dinosaurs came," Tanner continued. "And then they left, and then we had an Ice Age, and now... we're here."

"Very good," said Mimi. "Now, Grant, what kind of formation was the Falls of the Ohio, once upon a time?"

"It was part of a coral reef that stretched from here to Indianapolis!" he replied excitedly. "Which was not there 350 million years ago."

"And what kind of fossils can we find?" Mimi asked.

"Oooh! Fossils! Uncle Mike needs to see these." Christina and Grant's Uncle Mike was a paleontologist at the Field Museum in Chicago.

"I'm sure he has," Mimi said. "You tell me what's been found."

Grant, in his mind, prepared the list of fossils. He had a knack for remembering stuff like this. He must have gotten it from his Uncle Mike.

"Ready? Okay, we've got brachiopods, bryozoans, trilobites, and corals. Scientists have discovered more than 600 different kinds of plants and animals in five layers."

"Layers?" Mimi asked.

"Yes, ma'am," Grant said. "There are five different layers of fossils on the Falls."

"Ooh!" Christina interrupted, "you can also find hexagonaria—also known as 'Petoskey Stone,' the state fossil of Michigan."

"That's good, kids," Mimi said. "You're last, Sara. What can you tell us about the recent history of the Falls—say, within the last 200 years?"

"200 years? That's a lot!" Sara cried.

"Just be brief," Mimi said comfortingly. "Stick to the big events."

"All right... let's see... settlers first came to Kentucky in the 1770s," Sara began reciting. "The Falls have attracted curious people, scientists, and even explorers like Lewis and Clark, in 1803. The Portland Canal opened in 1830, with three locks at the end to drop steamboats and other boats down 26 feet. Later on, the Army Corps of Engineers upgraded the locks and built a dam. They're still improving the systems today."

"That's very good, all of you!" Mimi exclaimed. "Do you see how much you really remember? All you need is a little quiz at the end of a trip or visit, and you'll remember everything so well."

"Mimi," Grant said. "I just remembered that I'm hungry. It's time for our picnic!"

Christina was hungry, too, but what she really wanted was for Papa to get a call on his cell phone—a call from Charles, telling them that poor Lickety-Split had been found.

8 Paddle Wheels and Ferris Wheels

"Okay, kids," Papa said, "where shall we go to see the Great Steamboat Race?"

Christina and Grant winked at each other.

"How about Eva Bandman Park?" Christina suggested.

"Why there?" Mimi asked.

"Because they have a Ferris wheel there this year," Christina replied. "And you love Ferris wheels, Mimi!"

Mimi shook her head and smiled. "You know me too well. Papa, I guess that settles it! On to Eva Bandman Park!"

Papa drove the truck out of the Kentucky Fried Chicken parking lot and asked Mimi to give him directions.

Christina and Grant high-fived each other while balancing buckets of fried chicken on their laps. Christina glanced at her Carole Marsh Mysteries watch; it was now almost four o'clock. Another two hours, and—hopefully!—

they would have their next clue to help solve the mystery of the missing horse!

They finally spotted the Ferris wheel, slowly turning above the treetops, as they approached the park.

"Look at all the people!" Christina said, as they neared the park entrance. "I hope we can find a good spot to watch the race!"

And find Mr. Sunflower Seed, she thought. How are we going to do that? We don't even know what he looks like— or if he even is a *he*!

After parking the truck, the group carried their picnic dinner to an open picnic table near the giant Ferris wheel. As they spread out the fried chicken, mashed potatoes, coleslaw, beans, and biscuits, Mimi asked, "Who knows anything about the Great Steamboat Race?"

"I do!" Grant was the first to reply.

"Me, too!" Tanner said.

"Me three!" Christina joined in, and went back to watching the crowd for Mr. Sunflower Seed.

"Me four!" Sara said.

"It sounds like you won't need me," Papa said. He grabbed a crispy-coated chicken leg and began to eat.

"The first race was in 1963," Christina said. "It was between the *Belle of Louisville* and the *Delta Queen*." She

thought she saw someone acting suspicious over by the cotton candy cart, and someone else near the funnel cakes! Who *was* Mr. Sunflower Seed?

"The *Delta Queen* isn't even a real steamboat," Tanner said. "It runs on diesel engines."

"Where's the *Delta Queen* from?" Mimi asked.

"New Orleans!" Grant said. "It paddles its way up the Mississippi and Ohio Rivers just to take part in the race."

"There are three boats racing this year," Sara said. "The *Belle of Cincinnati* is joining the other two boats."

"Did you know that the race is frequently sabotaged?" Papa asked.

"It is?" Mimi said, surprised. "How?"

"The captains of the paddle wheelers try to do things that will lessen the other boat's chances of winning," Papa explained. "One time, the captain of the *Belle of Louisville* sent a whole bunch of really fat passengers over to the *Delta Queen* to slow the boat down!"

"You're kidding!" Grant said.

"I'm not kidding," Papa said.

"They have passengers on the boats during the race?" Christina asked.

"They sure do!" Tanner said. "People will do *anything* to get tickets to be on the boats for the race."

"How long is the race?" Mimi asked.

"It's 14 miles," Sara said. "The course starts at the Clark Memorial Bridge, just downriver from the Interstate 65 Kennedy Bridge. It goes upriver to the turnaround buoys at Six Mile Island, then goes back to the Kennedy Bridge. It takes about an hour and a half to finish the race."

"That sounds like plenty of time for a few rides on the Ferris wheel!" Grant said.

"Amen!" Mimi agreed. "All right, enough talk! Let's eat!"

As soon as they were finished with lunch and had deposited their trash in the trash cans, Papa ran to the SUV with the leftovers. Mimi herded the kids to the line to ride the Ferris wheel. Papa joined them in line with a handful of tickets. By the time they all got on for the ride, it was almost five o'clock.

"Wheeee!" Christina happily said. The car she rode in with Grant was the last to be filled, so the ride was going to be nonstop until passengers had to get off.

Up! Up! And away they went!

Christina kept searching the crowds for Mr. Sunflower Seed. "Do you see anything, Grant?" she asked.

"I sure do! Look at that view!" Grant said. He pointed straight ahead of them.

The Louisville skyline, highlighted by several tall

skyscrapers, rose above the trees. To its right, on the river, tucked under a big bridge—the Kennedy Bridge, for the interstate highway, Christina thought—were the three paddle wheelers, ready to start the race.

"Is it going to start now?" Grant asked.

Christina looked at her Carole Marsh Mysteries watch.

"In just a minute or two!" she said excitedly. Their car had reached the top of the Ferris wheel and it began to descend as the wheel kept turning.

"I hope we get back up to see the start of the race," Grant said, as the river disappeared from view.

"Me too," Christina said absently as she peered at the crowd below.

"Hey, Christina! Grant! Down here!"

They both looked down to see Tanner and Sara waving up at them from their car.

"We're going to see the start of the race!" Tanner shouted.

"Yay!" Grant yelled. "Whoo-hoo!"

The Ferris wheel kept on turning, and the three boats on the river came into view. Just as Christina and Grant re-spotted them, great plumes of smoke erupted from their smokestacks. The race was on!

"Which one is which?" Grant asked. He squinted and tried to tell.

"I don't know," Christina said. "Maybe they need to wear brightly colored silk shirts."

She laughed at her joke as their car began to descend. By the time they reached the top again, the paddle wheelers were just about to go under a small bridge upriver from the Kennedy Bridge.

"This is GREAT!!" Christina and Grant heard Mimi yell.

The Ferris wheel slowed down, and after Christina and Grant's car passed the boarding platform, it stopped. The riders in the car behind them got off, and new riders got on. This kept on until, at last, Christina and Grant had to leave their car.

"We got to watch the race a lot when we were stopped up on top of the Ferris wheel," Grant said to Mimi and Papa. "That was sooo cool!"

"It was way cool," Sara said.

"Let's go see if we can find a spot down at the riverbank to watch them race by," Papa suggested.

"Yeah!" Tanner shouted in agreement, and they all headed off for the riverbank—and the thousands of people already gathered.

Christina looked at her watch. It was now 5:24 p.m. "I hope we can find the meeting spot," she said to Grant. "But I don't even know where to start looking!"

9 PRELUDE TO A CLUE

Delta Queen had the lead—but not by much—as the three paddle wheelers cruised by. The *Belle of Louisville* was actually catching up. The *Belle of Cincinnati* seemed to be losing ground—or water, as they were boats.

The passengers on the boats were waving arms, legs, flags, shirts—anything they could wave, they waved it. They also yelled—loudly enough to be heard on the shore, and certainly on the other boats. Christina was sure that each boat's passengers were taunting the others.

"I've never seen a race this slow," Grant said.

"Me neither," said Christina.

"I have," Sara said. "Quite a few times, actually."

Eventually, the boats had gone far enough upriver to be obscured from view by the crowd and the trees at the river's edge.

"Let's go ride the Ferris wheel again!" Mimi said. She herded everyone back up the slight slope to the excitement of the carnival atmosphere.

Christina checked her watch. Ten until six. Oh, no! What will we do? Without another clue, it's hopeless!

As they threaded their way through the crowds of people, Tanner caught up to Christina.

"We're not going to find this meeting," he said sadly.

"But we have to," Christina said. "We have to save Lickety-Split!" She was on the verge of crying, because she felt sure that Tanner was right.

"We may have to just let the police find him," Sara said. Christina looked at her. Sara, it seemed, also felt they would miss the opportunity to be one step closer to finding the horse.

"Here we are, kids," Mimi announced. They had reached the line for the Ferris wheel. Christina looked around for anyone who looked as if they had stolen a horse this morning. But the dreadful truth was that there were too many people here, and they didn't know what the thief looked like.

"Papa, I'm thirsty," Grant said. "Can we go get something to drink?"

"I think so," Papa said. "Will you hold our place in line, Mimi?"

"Sure thing. You go ahead," she said.

Papa led the four kids to one of the many carnival food carts set up around the Ferris wheel. He picked one that didn't sell funnel cakes or corn dogs, just drinks and snacks.

Tanner and Sara waited by the fence surrounding the Ferris wheel while Christina, Grant, and Papa waited in one of the three lines at this cart. Grant stared at all the brightly colored snacks.

Christina looked at her watch one last time. Just a few minutes to go, she thought, and I'm stuck waiting in line to get a drink!

Finally, it was their turn to order. Grant asked for a giant raspberry slush. Christina half-heartedly asked for a bottle of water, as did Papa (only with a little more enthusiasm).

Christina looked at the man who stepped to the window in the next line over. He was wearing a bazillion Pegasus Pins on the straps of his overalls. He had a Polaroid camera hanging from its strap around his neck. He ordered a bottle of Coca-Cola.

It was then that Christina's heart jumped into her throat.

"I'd also like a bag of sunflower seeds," the man said.

10 A Clue in Blue... Overalls, That Is

Christina gulped.

Could that be him?!

Papa handed her the bottle of water she had asked for.

Oh, my gosh! Is it him?

"Let's get back in line," Papa said, and he led them away from the snack cart. Grant slurped his slushy as he followed Papa.

Christina followed, too, but kept looking back over her shoulder at the man in overalls. He casually walked over to a surprisingly vacant park bench facing the Ferris wheel, and sat down.

What do I do? Christina thought. Then she had an idea.

"Papa," Christina began, "I think I'll sit this one out."

"Really?" Papa said. "Okay. You and Grant go stand with Tanner and Sara over there. Mimi and I are going back on."

"Why don't you want to ride the Ferris wheel?" Grant asked. "Don't you want to see the steamboats from way up high again?"

"No, Grant, I don't," Christina answered. She waited until Papa had walked far away enough so he wouldn't hear them.

"It's that guy in overalls sitting on that bench!" Christina said excitedly, nodding her head in that direction. "At least, I hope it's him!"

Grant whirled to see. "That guy with all the pins?"

"Yes! He's got a Polaroid camera, and he bought a bag of sunflower seeds from the snack cart."

"Oh, man! What do we do?"

"We go get Tanner and Sara," Christina said, "and we go stand nearby."

Grant nodded excitedly. "Let's go do it!"

They walked as casually as they could—which wasn't easy, since their next clue might be sitting right over on that bench—over to Tanner and Sara. They were now between thirty and forty feet away from the bench, but the man was looking right at them!

"It's *him*!" Christina blurted.

"It's him *who*?" Sara asked.

"That guy on the bench," Grant said. "He's got a

Polaroid camera, and he bought a bag of sunflower seeds. See?"

Sara and Tanner looked at the overall-clad man. He had a brownish, untrimmed beard on his sunburned face. His brown hair was a bit of a mess, and it was flattened in a ring around his head, as if he had been wearing a hat. His Polaroid camera rested on his chest. He was also munching on sunflower seeds, splitting the shells with his fingers and popping the seeds into his mouth as fast as he could.

"He looks familiar," Sara said slowly. Christina knew she was thinking about where she could have seen him before.

"Not to me," Tanner said.

"Who's that?" Christina whispered. She pointed at a man who had suddenly appeared out of the crowd and was walking straight toward Mr. Sunflower Overalls.

The second man was sharply dressed—he wore a light gray suit with pinstripes and a red tie. He took off his light gray Fedora hat as he sat down.

"I know I've seen *him* before," Sara said. "I hope he doesn't recognize me!" She quickly stood behind Tanner.

"Who is it?" Tanner asked, shifting to better shield his cousin from view.

"I'm not sure, maybe a horse owner," Sara said.

"Grant, we have to go over there," Christina said. "We have to hear what they're saying."

Christina looked at the line for the Ferris wheel. Mimi and Papa were no longer in the line. They must be on there already, she thought. It's a good thing they're not paying attention. They wouldn't approve of their grandkids getting friendly with total strangers—especially strangers who might be thieves.

Tanner offered a bit of advice for their eavesdropping mission: "Go around to your left and sneak up behind them. They won't see you that way. We're going to find someplace else to stand."

With one last glance up at the Ferris wheel, Christina and Grant slipped into the crowd. They walked around the snack cart and ended up standing a few feet behind the men on the park bench. People occasionally walked between them and the bench. Christina felt it would be safe for them to stand there.

"I don't get why we can't just talk on the phone, man," the man in overalls said quietly. "Are we going to do this all the time?"

"Look, we can't have any evidence that ties you and me together," the man in the suit said. "If we talk on the phone, then the police might be able to connect us."

"Yeah, yeah, yeah," Mr. Sunflower Overalls said. "So what happens next?"

"The horse is safe?" said Mr. Suit.

"Yeah, of course!" Mr. Sunflower Overalls replied, his voice louder.

"Shhh," Mr. Suit said. Then, quietly, he said, "Keep your voice down. Tonight, you will move the horse to the second hideaway. Do you have the photo?"

Mr. Sunflower Overalls slipped a photo from his breast pocket and handed it to Mr. Suit. Christina saw it—Lickety-Split was standing in his trailer. She did not know exactly what a happy horse might look like, but she could tell that this was one unhappy horse.

His voice had gotten so quiet that it was hard for Christina and Grant to hear. They scooted closer and stood right behind the bench. Christina had the sense to face them away from the men.

"Good. Tomorrow," Mr. Suit said, very quietly, "I will send a note to his owners."

"What are you going to tell them?" Mr. Sunflower Overalls whispered.

"That their Thoroughbred is being held for a ransom of three million dollars," said Mr. Suit. "He will be held until after the Kentucky Derby, which should clear the way for

my favorite horse, Thai Spice, to win. If Thai Spice wins, I'll be nearly three million dollars richer—just from the bet I made. Even if Thai Spice loses, it won't be because of the Swamp Fox horse, and I'll still have three million dollars from the ransom."

"What if they don't pay up?"

"We meet tomorrow to discuss that," Mr. Suit said. "Be here tomorrow at 6 p.m. sharp!"

Be where?! Christina thought. She and Grant turned to see Mr. Suit hand Mr. Sunflower Overalls a small piece of paper. Christina recognized it—it was another betting slip. But it was folded—they couldn't read it!

Suddenly, Grant was bumped from behind and shoved forward into the back of the park bench. His blue raspberry slushy was crushed between his chest and Mr. Suit's back. A huge blue icy glob of slush flew up in the air—and landed right in Mr. Sunflower Overalls' lap!

Christina watched the betting slip dropped from Mr. Sunflower Overalls' hand and fall under the bench.

"What the—!" Mr. Sunflower Overalls jumped up from his seat and hurriedly brushed the melting ice from his overalls.

"What do you think you're doing, you klutz!" Mr. Suit yelled at Grant. Grant saw that Christina had a chance to

get the clue. So he started to back away—away from Mr. Suit, away from the bench, and away from the next clue.

Mr. Suit generously followed him.

"I-I-I'm, sorry, mister!" Grant stammered. "It's not my fault! Somebody pushed me!"

Christina glanced at Mr. Sunflower Overalls. He was completely turned away from the bench. She glanced at Mr. Suit. He was busy with Grant. Christina ducked down, snatched the slip of paper from the grass under the bench, and read it:

Pegasus Parade Review Stand, Th. 5 p.m.

She threw it back under the bench. Then Christina lunged upward, broke into a run, snatched Grant by the arm, and hauled herself and her little brother out of there as fast as she could!

11 THE FOG ROLLED IN OVERNIGHT

Tap tap tap.

Christina stirred in bed at the sound of something tapping.

Tap tap tap.

She yawned and stretched a big stretch. It sounded like something was tapping on a window pane.

Tap tap tap.

Christina opened one eye—the one nearest the window right next to her bed—and saw a big, black eye staring at her. Startled, she sat up in bed with a little yelp. Christina

looked with both eyes wide open, and saw a smiling Sara sitting on a horse outside her window. She held a riding crop in one hand while she waved with the other.

That's what was tapping on my window, Christina thought, a riding crop, the thin little stick that jockeys used to make their horses run faster.

Christina unlatched the window and threw up the sash. "Good morning, Sara," she sleepily greeted.

"Mornin'," Sara replied. "Are you ready to ride?"

"Oooh, not yet," Christina said. "I'm not even awake yet."

"Okay, then," Sara said. "I'll come back for you later. Get some breakfast." And with that, she tugged the reins away from the cabin, and gave the horse a little nudge with both heels. Sara's mount took off at a trot, and soon they had disappeared into the fog that had crept over Louisville and the surrounding areas overnight.

As least it's not as thick as pea soup today, Christina thought, as she let her body fall back into the soft sheets and pillows. Her eyes began to close.

"Hey, Tia," Grant mumbled, as he shuffled his way over to Christina's bed. "Was that Sara?"

"Yes, Grant."

"Was she riding a horse?"

"Yes, Grant."

"Was it a brown horse?"

"Yes, Grant."

"Can I ride it later?"

"Only if you stop asking me questions, Grant."

"Okay," Grant said, and he shuffled away. Christina heard him open the bedroom door and go out. Not long after that, the aroma of freshly-brewed coffee wafted its way into her nose.

That triggered a "Wake up, Christina!" call from her brain. Shortly after the coffee visited, the rich, sweet smell of biscuits baking practically threw the covers off the bed.

Christina padded out of the bedroom and made her way to the kitchen. Mimi, Papa, and Grant were already sitting at the table in the breakfast nook. The nook was shaped like an oval cut in half lengthwise, and there were no walls— just windows.

The bright sun was steadily burning off the fog, and the view from the breakfast table was amazing. Acres and acres of lush, green Kentucky bluegrass covered the rolling hills. White three-rail fencing followed the contours of the land, and horses seemed to be everywhere.

"Good morning, Christina," the chef said.

"Hi," Christina said.

"Well, if it isn't ol' sleepyhead," Papa greeted her. "Get enough shuteye?"

"Mmm-hmm," Christina hummed. She plopped down into a chair.

"Some orange juice? Or Ovaltine?" the chef asked.

"Ummm... both, please," Christina said.

Grant had already struck up an interesting conversation with Mimi and Papa.

"How come Sara doesn't have to go to school?"

"Sara's homeschooled," Mimi replied. She took a sip of her coffee. "Sara has things to do that are part of her daily routine—and part of her education."

"She didn't go to school yesterday," Grant said.

"Ha!" Papa exclaimed. "She sure did."

"What do you mean?" Grant asked.

"Well," Mimi said, "look at how much she learned—and how much she remembered she had learned before."

Grant cocked an eyebrow. He didn't quite understand.

"Think of it this way, Grant," Papa suggested, "everything that happened and every place she went yesterday was an educational experience."

"That's right," Mimi said.   "Even before sunup yesterday, she was learning how she, you, her father, and the police responded to a horse-napping. Then she—we all—learned more about the Kentucky Derby than we'd ever learned before."

"Then we went to the Falls," Christina helped. "We saw all those fossils."

"And got lessons in history, paleontology, and geology," Mimi said.

"Then we went to the Great Steamboat Race," Papa said, "and got another history lesson."

Not to mention how to go about solving a mystery, Christina thought to herself. That made her smile and perk up a little more.

"Good morning, everybody!" Sara called, as she entered the cabin's front door.

"Howdy!" Papa said.

"Sara, we were just talking about you," Mimi said.

"Saying good things, I hope," Sara said.

Christina and Grant waved—they were drinking their Ovaltine.

"Are you ready for your equestrian lessons?" Sara asked Christina and Grant. "I'm ready to teach you!"

"We'll be ready soon," Christina said. "We're going to eat breakfast first."

"Actually, we can start right now," Sara said.

"We can?" Grant asked, as the chef placed plates of neatly arranged eggs, biscuits, grits, and Kentucky ham in front of everyone.

They dug in without hesitation. Sara let them get a few bites and a few comments about how deliciously scrumptious everything was.

"Take a look at what I'm wearing," Sara said. "Notice anything different?"

Christina and Grant looked.

"You're wearing a helmet," Grant said.

"That's right," Sara said. She touched the helmet and ran her fingers across the brim. "This is called a hunt cap. It's got this peak in the front. A regular helmet doesn't have one."

"You're wearing gloves," Christina said. "They're to protect your hands from the leather reins, right?" Sara nodded yes.

"You don't have any laces on those really shiny boots," Grant said.

"You noticed," Sara grinned. "You don't want to have laces or buckles on your boots when you ride. You don't want anything to catch on the stirrups, just in case you have to dismount quickly."

"Where are your spurs?" Papa said with a chuckle.

Sara smirked and shook her head. "I don't wear spurs. Most people don't, except for showing and dressage. Some Western riders wear them. But I think spurs just hurt the horse."

Papa nodded in agreement.

"Spurs are cool," Grant said. "I like the jingly sound they make when you walk."

"Sara, what's *dressage*?" Mimi asked.

"Oooh, good question," Sara teased. "Dressage is a very complicated thing. You have to guide your horse through a course of markers. At certain markers, you have to guide your horse though certain maneuvers. It's very complex, and it takes a long time to master."

There was silence for a minute as everyone gobbled their breakfasts.

"What are those pads on the inside of your pant legs?" Christina eventually asked.

"These are special pants called *jodhpurs*," Sara explained. "They're tailored to be tight against your skin, but they're stretchy so you can easily move your legs." Sara reached down and pinched one leg of her jodhpurs at the knee. She pulled and tugged at the fabric to show them how stretchy it was.

"These pads protect your legs from rubbing against the saddle," Sara said. "You really do a lot of bouncing around when you're riding, especially if you're going faster than a trot."

"So, it's not a smooth ride?" Christina asked. Now that

she was fully awake, she was looking forward to getting her first riding lesson. But not if she was going to be bouncing around in the saddle!

Sara shook her head. "If you're just walking the horse, it's just a lot of swaying back and forth. Not much to think about. When you start trotting, which is a little faster than a walk, you have to learn how to sit in the saddle correctly and learn how to bounce with the horse."

"Geez! Sounds like it's easier to drive a car," Grant commented.

Sara scrunched her eyes up. "I don't think so."

"Definitely not," Papa said, and he wasn't smiling anymore. "Sure, it can be easy to drive a car—if there's no one else on the road with you. But once you get into traffic... give me a horse any day!"

"You can ride?" Sara asked.

"Shoot, darlin'. I grew up on a farm in Iowa," Papa said, smiling again. "I used to ride a horse to school some days."

"I think Papa could ride a horse and milk a cow at the same time," Christina said jokingly.

"Howww-dy!" Tanner called from the front door. The door opened, and Tanner ambled in. He, too, was dressed to ride, but his outfit looked nothing like Sara's.

"Now that's what I call dressed to ride!" Mimi said.

"Oh, yeah!" Grant agreed wholeheartedly

As Tanner walked toward the table, his spurs jingled, and the brown fringe on his legs swished all around. He took off his brown suede Fedora-style hat and nodded his head in greeting.

"Ladies, gents," he said.

"You've got spurs!" Grant said. "They sound sooo cool! Let me see 'em!"

Tanner turned around—the fringe on his legs swishing some more—and showed them the spurs on his boots.

"See," Tanner said, "the rowels—these little wheels—aren't very pointy, as you might have seen on some other spurs."

They all looked. Indeed, they weren't pointy at all. The rowels had just slight bumps on them.

"What do you have on your legs?" Christina asked. She knew she knew what they were called, but their name escaped her.

"These are chaps," Tanner answered, still turned around. "They don't have a seat. They just protect your legs from rubbing against the saddle."

"And they look cool," Grant said. "Look at all that fringe, man!"

"It's groovy!" Christina said.

"So are you ready to learn to ride?" Sara asked.

Christina and Grant looked at each other—there was nothing they could do about the mystery until later that afternoon.

"YEAH!" Christina and Grant shouted.

12 OH, HORSE TACK!

"Okay, you guys. How do I look?"

Christina came out of the bedroom wearing a hand-me-down pair of off-white jodhpurs with tiny little blue flowers, a hunt cap, and a pair of riding boots. She also wore a white blouse and a black leather vest.

Christina twirled on one heel so everyone could see. Papa hooted and hollered and Mimi oohed and aahed. Sara clapped her hands in approval.

"Yeehaw!" Grant yelled from the bedroom, and he pranced out. He emphasized every step to make sure his spurs jingled.

"Howdy, pardners," Grant said, stomping his way to stand next to his sister.

He was dressed just like Tanner, with boots, spurs, fringed chaps, and a hat.

"Hiyo, Silver!" Papa said.

"It's my little cowboy!" Mimi gushed.

"Awww... don't you look cuuute!" Christina teased.

"Looks like we're ready," Tanner said.

"Great! Let's go ride," Papa said. He stood and took Mimi's hand to help her up.

They all walked outside. Two horses, a chestnut pony and a roan pony, were tied to a fence rail. A bright yellow Jeep with the top removed was parked in front of the cabin.

"Tanner and I will ride our ponies over to the big barn," Sara said. "You guys follow in the Jeep."

Sara and Tanner untied their horses, and together they swung up into their saddles. They rode off side by side, and Christina, Grant, Papa and Mimi followed in the Jeep.

Christina and Grant watched the two horses canter along ahead of them.

"Boy, horses look funny from the rear end," Grant said. "It looks like they might trip over their own feet."

Papa laughed. "Yes, horses do look funny from this angle. And, you don't want to ride too close behind!"

When they reached the barn, Sara and Tanner dismounted and tied their horses to a fence rail.

"Wait here," Sara said. Then she and Tanner went into the barn. They came back out a minute later, each one leading a gorgeous pony.

"Okay," Sara said. She rubbed her horse's nose and said, "This is Hurricane. And that is Tornado."

"Cool names," Christina said.

"Now, let me tell you all about the tack," Sara said.

"The *tack*?" Grant asked. "You're not going to stick your horse, are you?"

"No, silly," Sara said. "Tack is the name for all the equipment you need for horseback riding."

"This is the saddle," she said, pointing to it. "There are many different kinds of saddles. These two horses are wearing roughout pony saddles. They're designed to help keep young riders in the saddle."

"My horse, Reesie, and Tanner's horse, Grapevine, are wearing dressage saddles, which have deeper seats. Your saddles have extended pommels," Sara said, pointing to the handle-like thing sticking up from the front of the saddle.

"Underneath the saddle," she continued, "we have a saddle pad. It absorbs the horse's sweat and keeps the saddle from irritating the horse's back."

"No irritation is a good thing," Christina said, elbowing Grant.

"Hey! I'm not irritating," he said in defense.

"Anyway, look at this," Sara said. She lifted a big flap hanging from the saddle, down the horse's side. "Under

the saddle flap is where we attach the girth. This leather strap goes under the horse's belly and attaches to the other side of the saddle. It keeps the saddle on the horse.

"Finally, we have the stirrups, into which you put your feet," Sara said. "These hang from underneath the pommel on adjustable straps. The stirrups on your horses are safety stirrups. They have a band on one side that will release if you happen to fall off your horse, so that your foot won't get caught."

Cowboy Grant looked at Cowboy Tanner and said, "Hey pardner, I'm itchin' to go *stir up* some dust!"

"Oh, brother," Christina moaned.

"Unnnhh," Sara moaned. "All right, let's look at the bridle." She pointed at the numerous straps crisscrossing the horse's head.

"This strap on top, behind the ears, is called the headstall," Sara said. "In front of the ears, on the horse's forehead, or brow, is the browband. And this strap, running from the headstall to the mouth, is the cheekpiece. Connecting the cheekpieces, we have the throatlatch, which goes under the jaw, and the noseband, which goes over the nose."

"Gosh! This is complicated," Christina commented.

"Have I lost you?" Sara asked.

Sarah's Tack Class

Parts of the Horse

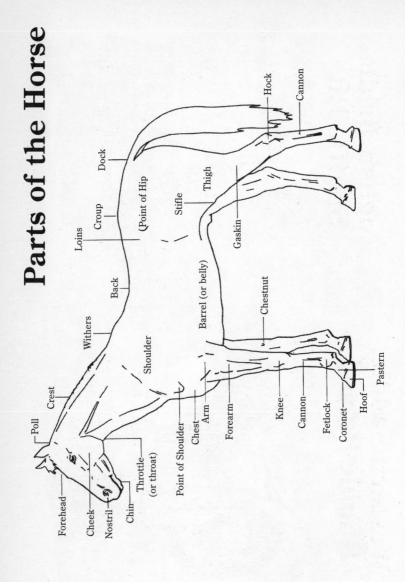

English Bridle, Snaffle Bit

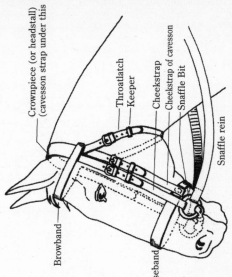

- Crownpiece (or headstall)
- (cavesson strap under this)
- Throatlatch
- Keeper
- Cheekstrap
- Cheekstrap of cavesson
- Snaffle Bit
- Snaffle rein
- Noseband
- Browband

Western Saddle, Double-Rigged

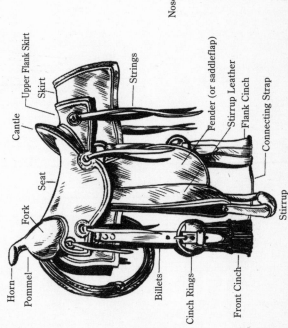

- Upper Flank Skirt
- Skirt
- Strings
- Cantle
- Seat
- Fork
- Pommel
- Horn
- Fender (or saddleflap)
- Stirrup Leather
- Flank Cinch
- Connecting Strap
- Stirrup
- Billets
- Cinch Rings
- Front Cinch

"No, it's just a lot to remember," Christina said.

"Well, I'm not giving you a quiz on this," Mimi said.

"Whew," Grant said, relieved.

"I'm giving you the quiz!" Papa said, and he laughed.

Hurricane snorted.

"Okay," Sara continued, "attached to each cheekpiece is the bit, which goes through the horse's mouth. There are lots of different kinds of bits, each shaped differently and with different features. Which one you use depends on what kind of riding you're doing."

"What kind of bit are you using?" Papa asked.

"For the riding we'll be doing, we use a rubber, loose ring, jointed snaffle bit," Sara said.

Papa nodded knowingly, but Christina, Grant, and even Mimi made funny faces.

"Don't worry about the kinds of bits," Sara said. "Whichever kind of bit you use, the reins are always attached directly to the bit rings. The reins are, basically, what you use to steer and stop the horse."

"And finally," Sara said, "we have one last bit of tack— the neck strap. This is a special piece of tack that inexperienced riders can hold onto if they feel uncomfortable. I've put them on your horses."

"Thanks," Christina said. "I'm totally inexperienced.

I'm looking forward to it, but I'll be a little frightened when I get up on that horse."

"Don't say 'horse', say 'pony'," Sara suggested. "It makes the horse seem smaller. And now, speaking of getting up there, let's show you how to mount a pony."

Sara walked over to her pony, Reesie, and untied her. She led Reesie over to her 'class', then turned sideways.

"Here's what you do—it's really simple," Sara said. "First, stand with your left shoulder next to your pony's left shoulder, and gather all the reins in your left hand. Next, you turn the stirrup around like this, three-quarters of a turn.

"Then, you put your left foot in—"

"—you take your left foot out..." Grant sang with a giggle.

"...you put your left foot in, and you shake it all about," Tanner sang along.

"You do the hokey-pokey and you turn yourself around," Christina joined in.

"That's what it's all about!" Mimi sang, turning herself around.

They all laughed so hard that the ponies got upset. The look in Hurricane's eyes reminded Christina of the scared Lickety-Split in the Polaroid photograph.

13 RIDERS UP!

When they had all settled down, including the ponies, Sara continued the lesson.

"Okay," she said, "Left shoulder to left shoulder, reins in left hand—got it?"

Everyone nodded.

"Okay, here's what will happen next," Sara said. "My left foot will go in the stirrup, and at the same time, I'll turn and grab the saddle with my right hand. Then I'll push off with my right leg, swing it way up and around, over the pony's rear, and sit in the saddle."

"Ready to see it?" she asked.

Everyone nodded. And in one swift, graceful motion, Sara was up in the saddle.

"Then you feel around for the other stirrup—without looking down—and slide your foot in. All done."

"Yay!" Christina and Grant applauded.

"To dismount, I do it the 'Australian' way," Sara said. "I take only my right foot out of its stirrup, then swing my leg back, up, and over the horse's rear, and step down with my other foot still in the stirrup. Just like this."

And in one swift, graceful motion, Sara was back standing on the ground.

"Christina? You ready?" Sara asked. Christina nodded. Papa moved closer to help, since Christina had never done this before.

Christina stood shoulder to shoulder with Hurricane. She thought, this animal is so much bigger than me! Christina took the leather reins from Sara. They felt thick and tough in her soft hands.

"Now, Christina," Sara said, "since you're a bit shorter than me, you may not be able to get your right leg over the pony using the stirrup. So I'm going to ask Papa to give you 'a leg up'."

"Sure thing!" Papa came over and stood on Christina's left side. "Bend your leg at the knee, darlin', and I'm going to push you right up the side of this pony. Don't think about going up, just think about getting your right leg over the pony without kicking him!"

Christina took a deep breath through her nose. Who'd

have imagined I'd be this nervous just getting up on a horse, she thought.

"Okay, here I go," Christina said, and she bent her left leg. Papa lifted her straight up. She swung her leg up and over the horse—and then she was in the saddle.

"OH!" Christina exclaimed. She was breathing fast. "This is pretty high up!" She was actually able to look down at Papa.

"Don't think about that," Papa said. "Just relax."

"That's right, Christina, just relax," Sara comforted her with a gentle hand on her leg. "It's a little weird at first, but you'll get used to it. Let's get your feet in the stirrups, and that'll help you keep your balance."

Sara was right. Once her feet were resting in the stirrups, Christina didn't feel as if she would fall off—until Hurricane moved underneath her.

"Aaah!" Christina cried. "Stay still, pony, stay still!" She gingerly reached forward and patted the pony's mane.

"It's okay," Sara said, "he's just adjusting to your weight."

Christina nodded nervously. She looked over at Grant's pony-for-the-day, Tornado. Suddenly, Grant's little body came shooting up the pony's side. He swung his leg over, just as he was shown, and landed squarely in the saddle.

"Whoa!" he said, looking down at the ground far, far below. "That was cool!" Then Tornado moved, actually taking two steps sideways, and nearly bumped into Hurricane. Grant, who had only one foot in the stirrups, started to slide right off the saddle.

But Papa pulled him back on.

"Whoa! That was not cool!" Grant said nervously.

14 RIDERS ON THE STORMS

"Sara, what kind of pony am I riding?" Christina asked. She and the rest of the group were walking down a dirt road through a stand of trees. The day had grown warm as the sun shooed away the fog. The sun peeked between the leaves of the trees above, dappling the road and the grass on either side with its light.

"Both Hurricane and Tornado are American Shetland ponies," Sara said. "They're related, you know—they were sired by the same stallion."

"American Shetland is the breed, right?" Grant asked. There had been no further problems with Tornado since the mounting incident, and Grant was thankful for that.

"Right," Sara replied. "We have about 20 different breeds on the farm, six of them ponies. The American Shetland is the smallest of those."

"They're called ponies because they're so small?" Christina asked. She had noticed some enormous horses on their way to the barn.

"That's correct," Sara answered. "A pony is any breed of horse that grows to less than 14.2 hands tall."

Grant held out one hand and looked between it and his horse. "I think my hand must be too small."

"It is, Grant," Tanner said. "A 'hand' is equal to about four inches."

Papa, riding a black Tennessee Walking Horse, chimed in, "Before people developed accurate measuring tools like rulers and tape measures, all they had to go by was what they had... well, on hand."

"Ohhhhh," Mimi moaned. "Very punny!" She had the pleasure of riding a charming spotted Appaloosa.

"Which is the biggest horse you have on the farm?" Christina asked.

"Umm... let me think," Sara said. "The biggest we have on the farm, though they're not our horses—they're just boarded here—are three English Shires. The biggest is almost 21 hands tall."

"That's huge!" Papa exclaimed.

"Do you measure to the top of the head?" Christina asked.

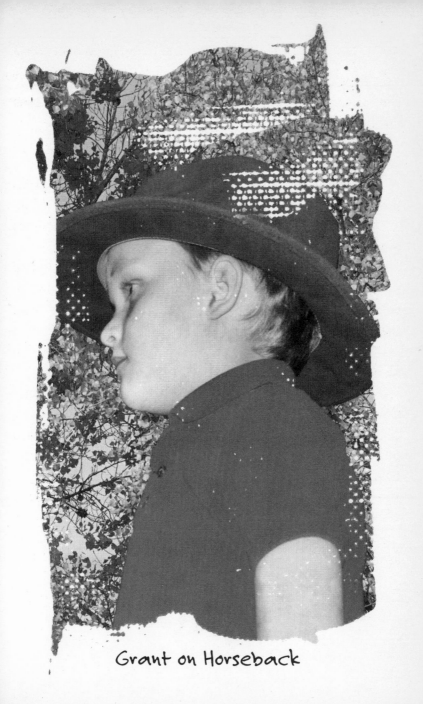

Grant on Horseback

"No, we measure from the foot to the withers—the highest point on a horse's shoulder," Sara replied. She patted Reesie's withers. "Reesie is a Welsh pony, and she stands 13 hands high."

"What kind of horse is Skit?" Papa asked.

"That's a trick question," Sara retorted. "He's a Thoroughbred, like all horses used mostly for racing."

"And just what makes a Thoroughbred a Thoroughbred?" Mimi asked. She asked in such a way that it seemed like she knew the answer.

"Oooh, that's a tough one," Sara said.

"Can I answer this one?" Tanner asked.

"Go right ahead, cuz," Sara said.

Tanner cleared his throat. "Historians are sure that it started way back in the late 1600s and early 1700s. There were three horses: the Darley Arabian, the Godolphin Arabian, and one other..."

"Byerley Turk," Papa whispered. He was riding alongside Tanner.

"...and the Byerley Turk," Tanner repeated. He continued, "In less than 100 years, the lines of lineage crossed enough times to develop an independent breed, called the Thoroughbred. What makes the breed so special is its ability to run very fast, sometimes for long periods of

time. That's called stamina."

"Tanner, that was an excellent explanation," Mimi praised. "How do you remember all that detail?"

Tanner shrugged his shoulders. "I read a lot."

"A LOT," Sara said.

"Living in horse country, especially Thoroughbred country, you read a lot about horses," Tanner explained.

"There's a paved road up ahead," Christina announced when she saw a car flash by beyond the trees.

"We'll be turning to ride alongside the fence," Sara said.

They left the dirt road, which turned in the opposite direction, and walked on the grass. Then, Christina got worried that the cars passing by would alarm the horses, or make them nervous. But thankfully, there were few cars on the road.

They rode on for a while in silence, which gave Christina time to think about their mystery. They had one missing horse—but not the right one (dumb thieves!)—being held for a ransom of three million dollars. The only clues she and her brother and Tanner and Sara could get were from these once-a-day meetings. She hated not being able to zip through the clues one after another and get the mystery over with.

But what can I do? We have to wait for the meetings,

Christina thought, and we have to make sure that we're there—especially today's meeting at the Pegasus Parade Review Stand!

"Say..." Sara said, "do you guys know what Skit's registered name is?"

"Registered name?" Christina asked. "What do you mean?"

"The name that's on his papers, and the name they'll use during the Kentucky Derby," Sara said. "We call him Skit for short."

"No, we don't know," Grant said. "But we've *nearly* found out several times!"

"Well, let me tell you a little story," Sara said. "See that intersection up ahead?"

They looked, and a few hundred yards ahead was a four-way intersection. Sort of. It was more like a fork in the road followed by a three-way intersection. It was not a pretty intersection, but, all around it were trees, grass, and white four-rail fences.

"'Skit' is short for 'Skittish', which is what we were going to call our Thoroughbred," Sara explained. "He was skittish around cars. But just cars, not trucks."

"Anyway," Sara continued, "we were bringing him home from the auction, and we came up that road on the left.

The main entrance to our farm is up that road on the right. When the truck and trailer made the tight turn to go to the farm, a wheel on the trailer clipped the bumper of a car that was stopped."

"So we stopped—with the trailer still out on the main road—to see what had happened. The driver of the car that came up behind us didn't expect us to stop like that, and that car hit the rear end of the trailer. Well, the next thing you know..." Sara sighed for dramatic effect.

"...the door on the trailer fell off. Somehow, Skit's halter broke and he was free to leave the trailer!"

"Let's stop here," Sara said. When everyone had stopped, she continued. "We found our horse unharmed, standing next to that road sign over there. And we decided that *that* should be his name."

"*What's* his name?" Grant asked, stumped.

"Read the sign..." Sara suggested.

15 DANGEROUS INTERSECTION

"Ha! You're kidding! That's the name of your horse?" Grant couldn't believe it. He giggled and giggled.

Mimi and Papa chuckled quietly (so as not to upset their horses).

Christina smiled from ear to ear. "I've wondered where people get some of these wacky horse names. Now I know!"

16 I Love a Parade!

"Oh, we're never going to get a parking spot around here!" Papa grumbled.

They were crawling their way through downtown Louisville, trying to find a place to park so they could watch the Pegasus Parade.

"This parade draws crowds of 200,000 people!" Mimi said. She turned to the four kids in the back seats. "Did you know that when they first held this parade in 1956, they did it with a budget of $640?"

Everyone shook their heads, no.

"Well, that's what it cost 48 years ago," Mimi said. "Today, the budget is almost $6 million!"

"So this is one kicked-up parade, eh?" Grant said.

Christina was hardly listening. She was getting very anxious to find a parking spot and get over to the Review

Stand—wherever that was—by five o'clock.

They *had* to get the next clue. Christina was worried about Lickety-Split—where was he? Was he all right? One thing confused the daylights out of Christina: why hadn't these guys realized that they horsenapped the wrong horse? She remembered that Sara had said that they were very similar—but there must be a way to tell them apart.

Besides, Christina thought, even if there wasn't, Dangerous Intersection would still have to practice on the Churchill Downs track. So, unless the horsenappers had absolutely no clue and were never at the track, they would know that they had the wrong horse.

Unless... Christina thought... unless they were at the track, and Charles was still playing a game with the horsenappers. He could be *breezing* Dangerous Intersection real early in the morning, under the cover of fog.

"Is that a parking lot we can use?" Papa asked.

"Where?" Christina said.

"Right where that truck's pulling in," Papa said. He pointed to a gated parking lot across the street. A man was standing at the entrance, letting only certain cars in, and waving others away.

Mimi opened the console between the front seats and took out a pair of binoculars. She trained them on the next

car that entered the parking lot. Then she smiled a mischievous smile.

"It's a parking lot for the news media," Mimi said. She opened her briefcase and set about looking for something. Neither Christina nor Grant could see, but they could hear her shuffling papers.

"Where is it? Where is it?" Mimi muttered to herself. "Aha!" She placed a white piece of paper on the dashboard.

Papa looked at the paper and laughed. "The old Bath Weekly News trick?"

"If it'll get us in there," Mimi said.

Papa turned into the parking lot entrance. The man looked at the paper on the dash. He peered into the front seat of the truck and waved them in.

"All right, Mimi!" Grant cheered.

In an amazing stroke of luck, the Review Stand—where parade performers stopped and strutted their stuff for judges, spectators, and TV cameras—was only two blocks away.

Mimi led them right to it. Amazingly, she and Papa found a clear spot to watch the parade from the front row. They unfolded the itsy-bitsy little tripod chairs they had brought along, and sat down.

Christina looked at her Carole Marsh Mysteries watch. It was still early for the parade, but they had less than

twenty minutes to go before the next meeting.

She looked at the Review Stand. It was a huge raised platform, like a stage, set between bleachers. There were television crews, photographers, journalists, and tables set up for judges. The bleachers were nearly full of spectators.

The sidewalks were also full of people, most looking for just the right spot from which to watch the parade.

"Christina, I think I just saw him!" Sara exclaimed. "It was Mr. Sunflower Overalls."

The four kids were standing on a concrete wall some distance from the street. They could see right over everybody's heads—except Grant, that is.

"Where?" Christina looked around wildly.

"See that red and yellow umbrella?" Sara pointed to a street vendor's cart with an umbrella over it.

"Yes."

"He's underneath it." Sara said.

"Probably buying more sunflower seeds," Tanner said.

"I can't see," Grant whined.

Three of them watched Mr. Sunflower Overalls leave the vendor's cart. He headed for the Review Stand. Christina noticed that he was wearing overalls with all the pins on the straps.

"Yeah! It's him!" Christina said. She wondered if those were the same overalls he had been wearing yesterday—*eeewww!*

"We've got to follow him," Grant said.

"No-o-o," Christina said warningly. "*We* can't follow him, Grant. He or the other guy—"

"—Mr. Suit?" Grant said.

"Yeah. One of them might recognize us from the incident at the park," Christina said.

"Oh, yeah," Grant remembered. "So who's going to go get the clue?"

Everyone looked at Tanner.

Sara said, "I can't go—I think he'd recognize me."

Tanner sighed. "All right. I guess I have no choice. What am I supposed to do?"

"Well," Christina said, "twice Mr. Suit has given Mr. Sunflower Overalls betting slips with meeting places and times. We could assume he'll do the same thing again."

"Okay, so how do I get the betting slip?"

"You don't have to get it," Christina said. "You just have to read it."

"All right," Tanner said. He sounded unsure about this one-man covert operation. "What time is it?"

Christina looked at her watch. "It's only three minutes

until five! Go! Get over there!" she shouted.

Tanner leapt from the wall and disappeared into the crowd.

Christina, Sara, and Grant (who had found another perch atop a taller cornerstone of the wall) watched a light gray Fedora hat move through the crowd. It was headed right for the Review Stand and Mr. Sunflower Overalls.

"Where's Tanner?" Sara wondered aloud.

Christina could only shake her head. She was too nervous to speak.

"There he is," Grant said.

"Where?"

"He just climbed up on the Review Stand," Grant pointed. "Right next to those two camera guys."

"Mr. Sunflower Overalls is right there, too," Sara said.

"And here comes Mr. Suit," Christina said. "At least he's on time."

Mr. Suit walked right up to his partner-in-crime. They talked for a minute, and all the while, Tanner was listening from above. Then the two men both looked down, as if they were looking at something in their hands.

Christina watched Tanner peering down at them out of the corner of his eye. He's being careful not to look straight at them, she thought.

One of the cameramen noticed Tanner standing behind them. He turned and yelled at Tanner, waving his arms to shoo him away. Surprised, Tanner backed away—forgetting that there was nothing behind him but a 10-foot fall. One more step backwards...

"Oh, no! He's going to fall!" Christina cried.

...and Tanner fell, his arms waving wildly in a useless try to grab hold of something.

Also startled, Mr. Suit and Mr. Sunflower Overalls looked up to see Tanner falling right toward them. Mr. Suit backed away (wimp! Christina later thought), but Mr. Sunflower Overalls stepped forward and caught Tanner in his arms.

Christina, Grant, and Sara watched a terrified Tanner say something to the big bear of a man, then scramble out of his arms. He disappeared into the crowd.

Mr. Suit and Mr. Sunflower Overalls talked for a minute more, and then they left.

"Did he get the clue?" Grant asked.

"Oh, gosh! I hope so!" Christina exclaimed.

"I hope so, too," Sara said.

17 BACK IN THE SADDLE AGAIN

Back at the horse farm, Christina, Grant, Tanner, and Sara waited for dinner outside the barn where Tornado and Hurricane were stabled. They watched the sun get lower in the sky, and talked about the third clue.

"They're meeting *where*?" Christina said, not believing what she heard.

"At Churchill Downs, Stable 13, tomorrow at 5:30 p.m.," Tanner repeated.

"That's half an hour before the Oaks," Sara said.

"What's the Oaks?" Christina asked.

"The Kentucky Oaks is the second biggest race of this weekend," Tanner answered. "It's a race just for fillies."

"Phillies?" Grant asked. "You mean the baseball team?"

Christina groaned. "No, Grant, a filly is a female horse."

"Actually, it's a female horse that has not reached

adulthood," Sara informed her.

"Huh?" Grant said. He squinted his eyes, something he often did when he was puzzled. "I'm puzzled."

"Okay, Grant, here's how it goes," Sara said. "When a horse is born, no matter if it's a boy or a girl, it's called a foal. Once it's about one year old, then it's called a filly if it's a girl, and a colt if it's a boy. Once they're four or more years old, girl horses are called mares, and boys are called stallions."

"Oh. That clears things up," Grant said.

"So how old is Dangerous Intersection?" Christina asked.

"He's three years old—just like all the other horses in the Derby," Sara answered.

A phone inside the barn rang. Sara excused herself and went to answer it.

"So the Kentucky Derby is only for three-year-old fillies and colts?" Grant asked.

"That's right," Tanner said. "But it's rare that a filly will run in the Derby. Usually, colts are bigger, stronger, and have more stamina."

"So Skit's special," Christina said. She was impressed, to say the least.

They fell silent and just watched the sun sink lower into the Kentucky sky. But soon, their thoughts went back to the mystery at hand.

Grant was the first to break the silence.

"What did they say about the ransom?" Grant asked. "What if Charles doesn't pay them three million dollars?"

"Nothing much," Tanner said. "Mr. Suit said they didn't expect to get an answer until tomorrow."

Christina said, "They still don't know that they have the wrong horse."

"I think they *do* know!" Sara said, coming out of the barn. She was very upset. "That was my dad on the phone."

"Sara, what's wrong?" Christina said. She slid off the fence and went over to her.

"I think they know now that they've got the wrong horse!" Sara exclaimed.

"How so?" Tanner asked.

"A little while ago," Sara explained calmly, "Earl was at the stables at Churchill Downs. Someone threw a rock at him—hit him right in the back."

"Ouch!" Grant said.

"There was a piece of paper wrapped around the rock," Sara continued. "The note on it said to pull Dangerous Intersection from the Derby, or we would never see Lickety-Split or our jockeys Fritz and Romeo ever again!"

"WHAT?!" Christina exclaimed. "How did they find out?"

Sara answered, "Thoroughbreds are required to have I.D. tattoos on the insides of their upper lip. Lead ponies don't."

"Why would they kidnap your jockeys?" Grant asked.

Sara looked at him. She was on the verge of tears. Christina saw it, too.

"Romeo and Fritz are *our* jockeys!" Sara exclaimed. "Maybe the bad guys stole a little more insurance that Skit won't be in the Derby. Without Fritz or Romeo to ride him, we can't race in the Derby!"

18 ROMEO, ROMEO, WHEREFORE ART THOU, ROMEO?

"I want to thank you for taking me with you everywhere this week," Sara said to Mimi and Papa. "I think it's helped me deal with all the trouble we've had."

"Well, Sara!" Mimi blushed. "I sincerely accept your thanks. But it is *we* who should be thanking *you* and your family for the heartwarming hospitality!"

"Oh, there's no need to thank us for that," Sara said.

"If you can thank me, then I can thank you," Mimi said. "Now hop up in there so we can go! We don't want to miss the Oaks!"

Sara clambered up into the SUV, followed by Tanner, then Christina and Grant.

They had spent most of the day at the Kentucky Horse Park in Lexington. After an early arrival, they visited the Man o' War Memorial and saw a special movie about

horses. Then they went on a horse-drawn trolley tour of the park, followed by a long tour of the International Museum of the Horse. They even had time to take a horseback ride. There was so much to see and do!

I have to come back here someday, Christina thought. Just not when we have so much mystery on our hands! Now they were headed back to Louisville to see the Oaks.

Christina looked out the window and watched the trees whizzing by in a blur. Suddenly, the trees ended and a white fence appeared alongside the road. There was a racetrack on the other side of the fence. A jockey was breezing a Thoroughbred on the track, and Papa slowed the SUV down to keep even with the running horse.

"Grant, look!" Christina said.

They watched the beautiful Thoroughbred gallop along. Its legs were a blur of motion, going from stretched out front and rear to coiled underneath its belly.

"It looks like it's barely touching the ground," Christina said softly.

I like the green, gold, and white colors of that jockey's silk, she thought, and the spider web pattern is really neat. Watching the jockey ride reminded Christina of Fritz and Romeo, Skit's jockeys. She wondered why the horse thieves decided to kidnap the jockeys when they learned

that they had the wrong horse.

Why not just threaten to harm the horse they had, Christina thought. Wouldn't that have been easier? Then she realized that the thieves wanted to let Charles know that they really meant business.

At the same time, Christina thought, the thieves made solving the mystery that much more important. Not only did she and her brother and their two new friends have to save Lickety-Split, they had to save two jockeys! Where were the jockeys being held?

And we don't have much time, Christina thought. We have two hours to get from Lexington to Louisville, and I don't think we've figured in extra traffic for the Derby Week events. We could be late, she thought. Oh, dear!

The racetrack turned away from the road, and the fence disappeared, to be replaced by trees. Papa was sure that they would get back with plenty of time to spare. Christina checked her watch—just a little less than two hours until the meeting at 5:30 p.m.

She settled in and opened one of the many books Mimi had just purchased. She hoped to read and remember a few things, but Christina was too worried that they wouldn't be back with enough time to spare.

19 OUT OF TIME!

Traffic was horrible—on the interstate highway, it moved at half of the speed limit. The streets of Louisville were as congested as the nose of a ten-year-old kid with a bad cold. The line of vehicles waiting to pass through the security gates had to be at least five miles long.

"This line has to be five miles long!" Christina said.

"I can see the gate, Christina," Mimi said. "We won't miss anything."

Ha! Nothing *important*! Christina thought. She was getting mad at the line of cars.

By the time they finally made it through the gates and headed for Dangerous Intersection's stable, it was 5:15 p.m. When they got to the stable, it was 5:20 p.m. And by the time Christina and Grant convinced Mimi and Papa that

they would rather stay at the stables than go watch the race, it was 5:25 p.m.

Christina glanced at her watch as they ran at a full gallop toward Stable 13. It was 5:30 p.m.! They skidded to a stop at the corner of a stable near Number 13. They all watched with great dismay as Mr. Suit and Mr. Sunflower Overalls parted from their conversation and went their separate ways. Mr. Sunflower Overalls put a betting slip in his pocket and walked out of sight.

"Oh, man!" Grant moaned.

"We're too late!" Sara cried.

"We'll never find them now!"

We're Too Late!

20 GRANT'S HOT ON THE TRAIL!

Christina stood there in disbelief. All her concentration was on the spot where the two men had been standing. She curled her lips in an angry snarl and stomped her foot into the dusty dirt. They had just lost their last chance to save Lickety-Split, Romeo, and Fritz—and put Dangerous Intersection back in the Kentucky Derby.

Sara was as much in shock as Christina. She remained standing where she had stopped. Her mouth was frozen in a big "OH NO!"

"This stinks," Grant said.

"Of all the rotten ways this could end, this had to be it," Tanner said.

Christina snapped out of her motionless state just in time to drag Sara out of the way of a horse-drawn cart that passed by. It was then that the hustle and bustle of

Churchill Downs on the day before the Kentucky Derby made them come back to their senses.

There were horses everywhere. They couldn't even turn around without a horse looking back at them with its big, black eyes. Jockeys were everywhere, too, their bright silks standing out from the colors in the crowds. Plus, there were plenty of other people, too, mingling throughout the stables, going about their horsey business.

"What are we going to do?" Sara moaned. "What *can* we do? We don't know where—or even if—they'll meet again!"

Sara let herself fall against the wall of the stable, and she slid down to the ground to a sitting position. Christina thought that looked like a good idea in spite of everything. So she slid down the wall, too.

For several minutes they sat and stood in silence. Christina looked at the other kids' very sad faces. This was so disappointing—to have been right on the edge of solving the mystery, and to have it swiped away by slow traffic.

Christina's thoughts turned back to Lickety-Split and the two jockeys. Where was that poor pony? Was she still tied up in her trailer? Had she been put in a stable somewhere? Was she still alive? Christina shivered at the thought of it. Lickety-Split was still alive—she just knew.

Poor Fritz and Romeo, Christina thought. I can barely

remember what Fritz looks like, and I've never met Romeo, but—oh, where are they?

From where she sat, Christina could see one of the secured entrance gates to the stable yards. There was a line of trucks pulling horse trailers waiting to get out. It looked like most of the trailers had horses in them.

Why are they waiting to get out? Christina thought. It's not like they have to pay for parking here. If a trailer was empty, the driver didn't have to stop. But if there was a horse in the trailer, the guards checked papers and the horses.

They're making sure nobody's stealing horses, Christina realized. Have they been doing that all along, or just since Lickety Split had been horsenapped? She asked Sara.

"It's always been like that," Sara replied. "For as long as I can remember."

So, Christina thought, you needed a horse's I.D to pass through security in order to get out. If you didn't have it, you weren't getting out...

...unless one of the guards was a bad apple and was in on your thievery! Otherwise, you were stuck in here, Christina thought. *If you couldn't get out, you were stuck in here.*

"Which means," Christina's thoughts escaped through her mouth, "that Lickety-Split might still be at Churchill Downs!"

"What?" Grant said.

"Where?" Tanner asked.

"I think Lickety-Split is still *here*!" Christina said excitedly.

"Here? At Churchill Downs?" Sara said. There was a hint of hope in her voice.

"Yes," Christina said. She got up from the dusty ground and helped Sara up, too. "Where can you hide a horse here?"

Grant's eyes popped wide open. He had the best idea! "Tia..."

Sara ignored him and gave Christina a that's-a-silly-question look. "There are only a thousand stalls here in these stables," Sara said.

"Christina," Grant prodded.

Tanner had a suggestion. "What if we followed Mr. Sunflower Overalls? If Lickety-Split is still here, then maybe he's going to check on her."

"But how will we follow him?" Sara asked. "We sat here for too long. There are too many people here—how could we find him?"

Grant couldn't stand it any more. "For Pete's sake! I know! I know!"

"What do you know, Grant?" Christina asked. She was trying to think, and Grant was interrupting.

"Follow me!" Grant shouted, and took off for the spot where Mr. Suit and Mr. Sunflower Overalls had had their meeting.

"I think we should follow him," Tanner suggested. He ran after Grant. Christina and Sara followed a moment later.

Grant had stopped, and he was looking at the ground. "See?" he said, and he pointed down.

They looked down. There were sunflower seed shells scattered all over.

"We can follow the trail of seeds!" Grant exclaimed. He walked away slowly, in the direction that Mr. Sunflower Overalls had gone. Christina thought he looked like a tiger stalking its prey, the way he was hunched low to the ground.

"He's a smart cookie," Christina mumbled. Then she grabbed Tanner and Sara each by an arm and said, "Let's go help him."

Grant pointed out a shell every few yards. So many people and horses were walking around that some of the shells were mashed into the dirt. But Grant spotted every one.

Eventually the trail led them to the stables all the way on the other side of the stable yard. Near the end, the trail appeared to lead directly to a stable that looked closed up. There was bright yellow DO NOT ENTER tape

crisscrossing the one door they could see.

A big white van was parked right next to it, so close that the passenger door would probably hit the wall of the building. The van had no windows except for the ones up front.

"Is that stable closed up for some reason?" Christina asked Sara. Christina looked and looked around for Mr. Sunflower Overalls, but couldn't see him.

"I seem to recall that there was a fire in that building a couple of weeks ago," Sara said. "It wasn't badly damaged, I guess."

"I think that's where Lickety-Split and your two jockeys are," Christina said. She could taste the sweet success of a mystery solved! And no one but I and my friends are going to finish this!

"Let's go get your horse back!" Christina said, and she dashed for the driver's side of the van. Grant, Sara, and Tanner followed in her wake.

"How can we get in there?" Christina wondered aloud as she stood with her back against the van.

Sara shrugged. "That side door is locked, I'll bet."

Grant and Tanner scooted around the back of the van. Five seconds later, they were back.

"Guess what," Grant said. "There's an open door on the other side of the van."

"Let's go!" Christina said. She led them around the van. Sara was right behind her, followed by Grant and Tanner.

Mr. Sunflower Overalls had left the double doors of the van open to block the view of the Dutch doors. Christina peeked around the doors. It was dark in there! Her eyes adjusted, and she realized that she was looking at a stall. She could almost see right through into the stable across the hall.

"Shhhh," Christina hushed. She took a deep breath, and entered the stable. It smelled like smoke in there, but not too badly. Christina tiptoed across the stall and peeked left—nothing. A peek right—and she saw a shadow move on the floor. It looked like a man was standing somewhere over there!

Christina listened carefully. It sounded as if someone was softly talking to a horse. The horse nickered softly. Christina tiptoed out of the stall and crept down the hall. Sara, Grant, and Tanner quietly followed her.

When all of a sudden, Mr. Sunflower Overalls stepped backward from a stall and crossed right in front of Christina!

Startled, he jumped. Then he looked at Christina...

"I remember you! And you!" he said, pointing at Christina and Grant. "You spilled that drink on me at the park! And you!" he said, pointing at Tanner, "... you're the

one who fell off the Review Stand yesterday!

"I'm going to get you!" He turned and raised his big arms and started after them.

"Oh, no you're not!" Christina said, and she turned to get out of there. She got one step before she plowed into the other kids. In that one second, Mr. Sunflower Overalls had closed on them, and was readying his giant arms to scoop them all up!

"HOLD IT RIGHT THERE!" a very loud, very "I-mean-it!" voice shouted.

Christina looked up to see a security guard standing down the hallway. Two more entered and stood by his side.

She looked back at Mr. Sunflower Overalls. He was slowly putting his hands up the air.

Christina thought, he's been caught, and he knows it! Yeah!

She glanced into the stall, and saw a horse that looked very much like Dangerous Intersection. Tied up and tossed into the hay were Fritz and Romeo, the jockeys.

Christina ran to the security guard.

"Officer! Officer! WE found the missing horse and the jockeys!"

21 AND THEY'RE OFF!

"Whose hat is the best?!" Mimi asked.

"Yours is!" Christina and Grant cheered.

"Whose?"

"Yours!"

"That's right! Wheee!" Mimi said, as she grabbed hold of her red, lace-trimmed, umbrella-size hat. A gust of wind threatened to turn it into a parachute.

Papa, ever the gentleman, helped Mimi keep her hat from becoming airborne. He was dressed in a fine black tuxedo, with a white, red-banded straw fedora.

Grant wore the exact same thing. Christina wore a twilight-blue gown and a matching hat. Sara and Tanner were both finely dressed in gown and tuxedo.

In the Churchill Downs grandstand were thousands of spectators and thousands of hats—oh, what a sight!

127

"LADIES AND GENTLEMEN," the announcer said over the public address system, "PLEASE RISE FOR THE SINGING OF THE NATIONAL ANTHEM."

Everyone rose to their feet. All the men, and some of the ladies, took off their hats. As the song played, Christina noticed that absolutely everyone had stopped to honor the flag. How patriotic, she thought.

Twenty minutes later, after the bugler bugled the "Call to the Post," the crowd erupted in cheers. The sleek, shiny Thoroughbreds began the post parade out of the tunnel and onto the track. The band struck up the traditional "My Old Kentucky Home," the state song of Kentucky, played and sung at the Kentucky Derby since 1930:

> *The sun shines bright in the old Kentucky home,*
> *Tis summer, the people are gay;*
> *The corn-top's ripe and the meadow's in the bloom*
> *While the birds make music all the day.*
> *The young folks roll on the little cabin floor*
> *All merry, all happy and bright;*
> *By'n by hard times comes a knocking at the door*
> *Then my old Kentucky home, Good-night!*
> *Weep no more my lady. Oh! Weep no more today!*
> *We will sing one song for my old Kentucky home*
> *For the old Kentucky home, far away.*

Ten minutes later, all the horses stood in the gate, ready to be unleashed. The announcer called out, "It is now post time!"

Just seconds later, when all the horses were just right, the starting bell sounded—and 13 incredible racehorses exploded from the gate!

"AND THEY'RE OFF!" The track announcer kept everyone informed of the progress of the race as they galloped up the first stretch. Giant TV screens in the infield gave a close-up view of the racers.

The horses passed in front of Christina's and Grant's seats. Dangerous Intersection was holding his pace steady with the field. The horses flew by at about 30 miles per hour, as fast as a car on a city street. But it sounded like no car on earth. It was a low, rich, thunderous noise that glided by on a flurry of hooves.

Charles, along with Earl, was watching from two rows back in the box seats. Earl had told them to watch for her to make a mid-race surge to third place, then another surge to the front up the stretch.

"Coming around at the three-quarter-mile, it's Lazy Bones with the lead, Radio Flyer on his quarter, and Price Is Right trailing by half a length. Jack Be Quick holding onto fourth ahead of Thai Spice, then Dangerous Intersection..."

The field hurtled down the backstretch.

"Radio Flyer falling back, Price Is Right gaining on Lazy Bones. Dangerous Intersection is making a charge up the backstretch, pulling ahead of Thai Spice and now passing Jack Be Quick..."

The field entered the turn at the three-eighths mile post.

"And now it's Lazy Bones fading to second, Radio Flyer is back in seventh, far away from the lead. Deep in the turn, it's Price is Right with the lead, then Lazy Bones and Dangerous Intersection. Now Unexpected is starting a charge! Driving up on the outside, making it a three-horse battle with Thai Spice and Jack Be Quick.

"Past the one-quarter mile, and DOWN THE STRETCH THEY COME! Unexpected and Thai Spice surging ahead! Lazy Bones trying for the lead again! Dangerous Intersection behind by two lengths, with Thai Spice and Unexpected gaining fast!

"Price Is Right is fading! Lazy Bones has the lead again, Thai Spice now alongside Dangerous Intersection. One-eighth-mile, and Dangerous Intersection is making a STRONG surge to the front! It's Dangerous Intersection,

pulling away from Lazy Bones and Thai Spice! Unexpected is trying for second—and it's Dangerous Intersection winning the Kentucky Derby by a full length!"

"YAAAAYYYYYY!!!" cheered the spectators. The kids exchanged high-fives. Charles reached out to them amidst the congratulations he was getting.

"You kids saved the day!" Charles exclaimed. "I hope you bet on the winner."

"Bet—we forgot to bet!" Papa said.

"Well, that's what you get," Grant said.

"Get for what?" Papa asked.

Grant smiled. "For horsin' around!"

Everyone laughed.

"Come on, folks!" Charles said. "To the Winner's Circle!"

THE KENTUCKY DERBY

Places To Go & Things To Know!

CONNECTIONS

Louisville, Kentucky – city on the northern border of Kentucky, on the Ohio River, founded in 1778 by George Rogers Clark

Churchill Downs, Louisville, KY – home of the Kentucky Derby, the track was built by Colonel Meriwether Lewis Clark (grandson of William Clark); it formally opened in 1875–the first three races were the Clark Handicap, the Kentucky Oaks, and the Kentucky Derby

The Kentucky Derby Museum, Churchill Downs – if you can't make it to the Kentucky Derby, this really is the next best thing; make sure you see the 360-degree panoramic movie, "The Greatest Race"

J.B. Speed Art Museum – founded in 1925 by Hattie Bishop Speed as a memorial to her philanthropist husband, James Breckenridge Speed; the museum's collection focuses on Western art; annual attendance is nearly 200,000 visitors per year

Louisville Slugger Museum – tour the factory and see how the most famous bats in all of baseball are made; see the collection of priceless pieces of baseball history; go and have a ball!

Louisville Slugger Park – home to Minor League Baseball's AAA team the Louisville Bats

Louisville Zoo – go see the animals!

The Belle of Louisville, Waterfront Park, Louisville – the oldest operating steamboat paddle wheeler in the U.S. is a National Historic Landmark that can take you on a sightseeing cruise on the Ohio River (but only from Memorial Day to Labor Day!)

Kentucky Horse Park, Lexington, KY – this working 1,200 acres horse farm is surrounded by 30 miles of white plank fence; features tours of the farm, the International Museum of the Horse, and the Man O' War Memorial

Falls of the Ohio and Interpretive Center, Clarksville, Indiana – tour the exhibits and explore the Falls; see what life was like 350 million years ago

The Kentucky Derby – more than just a horse race held on the first weekend in May every year since 1875, it is now a week-long festival of events culminating in the greatest two minutes in all of sports

ABOUT THE AUTHOR

Carole Marsh is an author and publisher who has written many works of fiction and non-fiction for young readers. She travels throughout the United States and around the world to research her books. In 1979 Carole Marsh was named Communicator of the Year for her corporate communications work with major national and international corporations.

Marsh is the founder and CEO of Gallopade International, established in 1979. Today, Gallopade International is widely recognized as a leading source of educational materials for every state and many countries. Marsh and Gallopade were recipients of the 2004 Teachers' Choice Award. Marsh has written more than 16 Carole Marsh Mysteries™. Years ago, her children, Michele and Michael, were the original characters in her mystery books. Today, they continue the Carole Marsh Books tradition by working at Gallopade. By adding grandchildren Grant and Christina as new mystery characters, she has continued the tradition for a third generation.

Ms. Marsh welcomes correspondence from her readers. You can e-mail her at carole@gallopade.com, visit the carolemarshmysteries.com website, or write to her in care of Gallopade International, P.O. Box 2779, Peachtree City, Georgia, 30269 USA.

IT'S A HORSE, OF COURSE GLOSSARY

Bridle: the assembly of straps that fit around a horse's head, used for riding

Canter: faster than a trot, but slower and smoother than a gallop

Colt: a male horse that is between one and four years old

Filly: a female horse that is between one and four years old

Foal: a baby horse under one year old

Gallop: running as fast a horse can run

Halter: an assembly of straps that fit around a horse's head, used when leading or transporting a horse

Jodhpurs (jod-purrs): special pants worn by horseback riders; they are made of tight-fitting stretchy fabric, and feature extra padding on the insides of the legs

Locks: a system of "water elevators" that raise and lower boats past drops in rivers

Mare: a female horse four or more years old.

Nicker: a low, soft, grunt-like sound

Paleontologist: a scientist that studies fossils to learn about life in the past

Philanthropist: someone who donates large amounts of money to charitable causes

Pony: a member of any breed of horse that typically grows to less than 14.2 hands high (56.8 inches)

Stallion: a male horse four or more years old

Supercontinent: what the earth's continents are called when they were one solid land mass, 300 million years ago

Tack: all the equipment needed to safely ride a horse, includes the bridle, reins, and saddle

Trot: a horse's speed that's slightly faster than walking

Whinny: a loud, high-pitched, squeal-like sound

Yearling: a one-year-old horse

SCAVENGER HUNT

Recipe for fun: Read the book, take a tour, find the items on this list and check them off! (Hint: Look high and low!) *Teachers: you have permission to reproduce these pages for your students.*

1. Derby Museum

2. Julie Krone

3. Fossils

4. Man O' War Memorial

5. Pegasus Parade

6. Saddlecloth

7. Appaloosa

8. Heartbreak Lane

9. Filson Historical Society

10. Lexington

BIBLIOGRAPHY

Baker, Kent *The Horse Library: Throroughbred Racing* 2002 Chelsea House Publishers J 798.4

Coggins, Jack *The Horseman's Bible* 1966 Doubleday & Co., Inc.

Edwards, Elwyn Hartley, Ed. *Encyclopedia of the Horse* 1977 Octopus Book Ltd.

Green, Lucinda *DK Superguides: Riding* 1993/2000 Dorling Kindersley 798.23

Hirsch, Joe and Bolus, Jim *Kentucky Derby: A Chance of a Lifetime* 1988 McGraw-Hill 798.4

Holub, Joan, *Why Do Horses Neigh?* 2003 Puffin Easy-to-Read

Humphreys, John O. *American Racetracks and Contemporary Racing Art* 1966 South Bend Publishing Co., Inc. 798.403

McBane, Susan *Understanding Your Horse* 1992 Ward Lock Books/Ward Lock Riding School 636.1

Silver, Caroline *World of Horses in Full Color* 1983 Omega Books Ltd. 636.1

Stewart, Gail B. *Learning About Horses: The Thoroughbred Horse: Born To Run* 1995 Capstone Press J 636.1

WRITE YOUR OWN MYSTERY!

Make up a dramatic title!

You can pick four real kid characters!

Select a real place for the story's setting!

Try writing your first draft!

Edit your first draft!

Read your final draft aloud!

You can add art, photos or illustrations!

Share your book with others and send me a copy!

SIX SECRET WRITING TIPS FROM CAROLE MARSH!

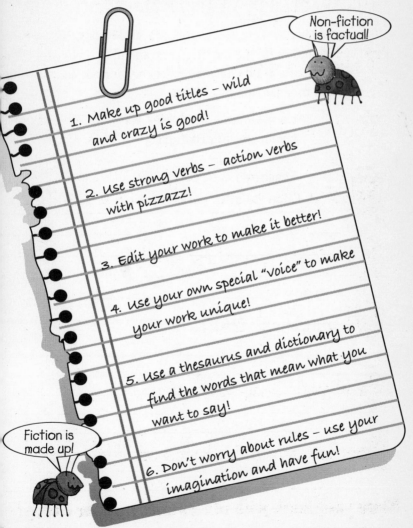

Non-fiction is factual!

1. Make up good titles – wild and crazy is good!

2. Use strong verbs – action verbs with pizzazz!

3. Edit your work to make it better!

4. Use your own special "voice" to make your work unique!

5. Use a thesaurus and dictionary to find the words that mean what you want to say!

Fiction is made up!

6. Don't worry about rules – use your imagination and have fun!

WOULD YOU LIKE TO BE A CHARACTER IN A CAROLE MARSH MYSTERY?

If you would like to star in a Carole Marsh Mystery, fill out the form below and write a 25-word paragraph about why you think you would make a good character! Once you're done, ask your mom or dad to send this page to:

> Carole Marsh Mysteries Fan Club
> Gallopade International
> P.O. Box 2779
> Peachtree City, GA 30269

My name is: _____

I am a: ____boy ____ girl   Age: _____

I live at: _____

City: _____   State:____ Zip code: _____

My e-mail address: _____

My phone number is: _____

_____

_____

_____

_____

_____

_____

_____

_____

_____

_____

Enjoy this exciting excerpt from

THE MYSTERY IN THE ROCKY MOUNTAINS

1 WHAT A POINTY AIRPORT

"Let's see," said Christina, with a big yawn. "I looked out the window over Georgia, Tennessee, and Missouri. I ate over Kansas. And I slept over . . . well, I guess I don't know what I slept over, but isn't it time to BE THERE?" She squirmed beneath her snug seatbelt.

Her grandmother, Mimi, gently rubbed the top of Christina's soft, brown hair. "I know it's been a long ride," she agreed.

"But we've begun our descent and are just about to come in for our landing," Christina's grandfather, Papa, told her. Papa had his own pilot's license and his own cute, little red airplane, so he knew a lot about aviation stuff.

Christina shook her younger brother, Grant. "Wake

up! Wake up!" she warned him. "We're coming down!"

Grant sat up with a start. His naturally curly hair stood on end in several places as if a cow had licked its way across his head. "Down? DOWN?!" he muttered loud, then louder, as he rubbed his eyes and looked out the window of the Boeing 767.

"She means we're about to land," Mimi reassured him.

"Oh," said Grant, stretching. He pressed his nose flat against the cold window. "Hey, we're landing in the mountains!"

That comment made Mimi, Papa, Christina—and everyone nearby—stare out of the plane.

Papa shook his head. "I don't see what you mean, Grant."

Grant pointed downward. "See all the pointy, white peaks. That little mountain range."

Papa laughed; so did everyone else. Grant folded his arms across his chest and scowled. What had he said that was so funny, he wondered.

Mimi knew Grant was embarrassed. She patted him on the shoulder. "You're right, Grant. The Denver International Airport does look like a miniature mountain range, doesn't it? They made it in that style on purpose. The big tent peaks make you think of the famous Rocky Mountains."

Grant smiled, as if he knew that all along. Then, Christina pointed out the window and said, "Now THAT'S a mountain range!"

Everyone looked out at the sawtooth silhouette of a strip of endless white mountains covered in snow against a bright blue sky. It was beautiful.

Mimi laughed. "You're right! The Rocky Mountains are one of the most amazing and beautiful mountain ranges in the world. Even though I've written a lot about geology, it's still a mystery to me how something so majestic got created."

Christina frowned and cleared her throat. "Mimi," she said sternly, glaring at her grandmother from beneath arched eyebrows that seemed to say, *remember*?

"What?" asked Mimi, pretending to be aggravated, but Christina and Grant knew that she understood perfectly well what was meant. "WHAT?" Mimi repeated, teasing them.

Christina shook her head, her long brown hair slinging back and forth. "Don't even use that word!"

"What word?" Papa asked.

"What word?" Mimi asked.

Grant laughed. "The M-word!" he said. "Mystery!"

Christina scrunched back in her seat. Mimi was a kid's mystery book writer. She and Grant were lucky to get to travel with their grandparents on research and writing trips, but somehow, Mimi almost always got involved in a real, live mystery. And, it always seemed like it was up to Christina and Grant to solve it.

Mimi just smiled, her blond hair sticking up like

little mountain peaks. She continued to chew on her red
marker pen while she pondered the yellow legal pad in
her lap. "I have no idea what you're talking about," she
said sweetly.

"Sure!" grumbled Christina.

"SURE!" repeated Grant.

"Hey, this is a winter vacation," Papa reminded
them. "No mystery necessary."

"Welcome to Denver, the Mile High City!" the pilot
said over the intercom system. *"We will be landing in a
moment. It is sixteen degrees outside, so put on your winter
duds, folks. Don't break a leg on the ski slopes. And come
back to see us again, real soon, you hear?"*

www.carolemarshmysteries.com

- *Check out what's coming up next! Are we coming to your area with our next book release? Maybe you can have your book signed by the author!*

- *Join the Carole Marsh Mysteries Fan Club!*

- *Apply for the chance to be a character in an upcoming Carole Marsh Mystery!*

- *Learn how to write your own mystery!*